RAT TALES

A MISCHIEF OF LITTLE HORRORS

P. A. RUDDERS

Rat

Tales

A Mischief of Little Horrors

*

P.A. Rudders

Contents

:

About the author

P.A. Rudders was born in London, England. Having now retired to the Welsh mountains to enjoy various outdoor pursuits, he is also pursuing his creative writing interests. He is a prolific blogger, book reviewer, and is a co-founder of the IASD writing site/group, to help, support, and encourage new writers.

www.indieauthorsupportanddiscussion.com

www.rudderswriting.com

www.thecreaturetales.com

P.A. Rudders has had several 'guest' stories published in other short story collections, including *You're Not Alone,* by Ian D. Moore (in aid of Macmillan cancer charity), *The Welcome,* a sci-fi anthology by Tom Benson, and *Holes: An anthology of Indie authors.*

This latest anthology, *Rat Tales*, is the first of a three-book collection, *The Creature Tales,* with books two and three scheduled for publication early 2019.

Several *Rat Tales* novels to complement this anthology are in the planning stage.

<u>Contact:</u> echoesofthepen@gmail.com

Acknowledgements

Huge thanks to my beta readers for taking the time to read through my stories before publication, for being honest enough to tell me what bits they liked, and more importantly, those bits they thought were utter rubbish, my son and best mate being especially vocal in the latter! I mean, who needs enemies with friends and family like that? (only kidding, guys, you both rock!).

Thanks also to Sharon Brownlie of Aspirecovers.com for her help and advice in the design of my cover for this first instalment of my Creature Tales collection.

And lastly, a huge thanks goes out to all my fellow members of the IASD for their continuing help, advice, and encouragement!

<u>Preface:</u>

Horror wouldn't typically be my first port of call when deciding what to read and even less so when it comes to writing. Why then a collection of blood and gore filled rodent horror stories? Well, I still remember just how impressed and fascinated I was when I first read James Herbert's Rats trilogy. For me, that was horror in its purest form - no demons, mythical monsters, or recanting spells on some altar in the woods at midnight, but instead, real flesh and blood creatures.

I would say 99% of the population have an irrational but inbuilt revulsion of rats despite most of us rarely being more than a few hundred feet or so from the nearest one no matter how out of sight we think they might be - what better theme then for the budding horror writer?

I don't think it's possible to improve on James Herbert's original format, but short stories though, that's a different matter. The short story genre allows the writer to explore any number of ideas while still sticking to a central theme if they want, which is what I've tried to do here. I hope you enjoy …

~ x ~

Dark Eyes

"Bloody rats!" Jack roared, partly in anger but mostly from a mixture of fear and loathing of the vile vermin, mesmerised almost as one the size of a small cat scurried across his path. Several more darted about in all directions, nearly tripping him up in the process before making their escape through the half-open barn door. But the sheer number, perhaps he should be the one making *his* escape, Jack thought. He watched one lone rat turn, and just for a moment, stop and look up at him before turning again to run and join his many brothers and sisters. Jack would later swear he could see pure hate-filled evil in those darkened eyes, but for now, his only concern was for his family and the farm.

He'd tried all the usual rodent poisons, legal or otherwise. Sarah, Jack's wife, hadn't been too happy with the 'or otherwise.' Being brought up in a town, she still had many of the townspeople's more gentle and sentimental attitudes towards animals and nature. She insisted there must be more humane ways of dealing with their local rat problem, ones that didn't include poisoning, gas, or any other solution she saw as the farmer's equivalent of a weapon of mass destruction. In the end, her objections had been irrelevant. Jack's efforts trying to kill them in large numbers had so far proved useless; either the rats were getting smarter, or they were becoming immune to the common over the counter remedies.

It was time for something different. Jack recalled reading somewhere that rats were cannibals, or at least prone to it sometimes for reasons he didn't remember. It was that single memory that had given him the idea - what if he could use that otherwise repugnant trait to reduce the excess number of rats with a few ravenous cannibalistic ones? Some part of him liked the idea of getting the little bastards to kill each other off. First though he would have to capture a few, well, about a dozen or so.

Like before when he had tried laying poisoned bait for them, ineffectively as it turned out, he left more of the same only this time laced with ground-up sleeping pills. Nothing poisonous or fatal that Sarah could reasonably object to, just something he hoped would knock them out long enough to carry out the next phase of his plan. The following morning, that part of Jack's plan had worked - there lying scattered about the barn were about twenty sleeping rats, eight of which he immediately finished off with a pitchfork. The remaining twelve he strung up upside down by their tails from one of the rafters, carefully spaced so that each rat was just within swinging distance of the next. After a few hours, they started to regain consciousness. At first, they frantically jerked and swung from side to side, probably due to a combination of fear and confusion. They were angry at their mistreatment, and relying mostly on their tails for balance, being strung up like that panicked and disorientated them further.

As the hours and then days passed, that anger and panic became something frighteningly different, an almost frenzied need for food and water. With no other source of nourishment to hand it soon became a matter of dog eat dog, or in this case - 'rat eat rat.'

Rats had often eaten one another in the past to survive but only as nature's way of combating famine or over-crowding. What they were forced into doing now was worse ... *much* worse.

Three days later just four of the original twelve were still alive. The strongest and most vicious had survived by swinging and clawing away at the living and soon after, lifeless, mutilated bodies of the weaker adjacent ones.

Despite their now thinner and wretched state, Jack was more than a little afraid when he approached them. It was a sight he hoped never to see again yet felt powerless to turn away from, watching the four remaining live ones hiss and spit the closer he got. One was bigger than the other three by quite a margin and judging from the way it was still thrashing about, equally stronger too. Then he realised - it was the same one that had looked up at him, the one with the dark hate-filled eyes. Jack shuddered. All four rats focused on him. It was *his* blood and flesh they could now smell, had a taste for it - if fear did have an odour, Jack knew he must have reeked of it.

He thought for a moment. His gut feeling was it might be best to abandon the scheme, to put the wretched creatures out of their misery there and then. A few whacks with a shovel at their limp, tired bodies and that would be it. But apart from removing the hissing hate-filled ones in front of him, what would that solve? He knew there were hordes more waiting in the wild?

Jack wanted - no - *had* to be rid of them if his farm was to survive. He had to close his eyes to break the rats' hold on his gaze before shuffling through the hay to open the barn door in readiness for their escape. On the way back, he grabbed hold of a field-scythe.

Jack stood several feet back from the rats' hanging bodies. He looked hard at them before taking a lunging swing at the thin wires from which the rats were still suspended. All four were hissing and spitting their hatred for their human tormentor. To the rats or anyone who might have been watching, Jack would have cut an impressive image as the grim reaper at that moment.

Jack watched them crash to the floor with a thud the instant the razor-sharp edge of the scythe sliced the space between the rafters and the ends of the rats' tails. He edged back a little, watching them from a dozen or so feet away. Jack had expected the live ones to make a lightning dash for the open barn door. They didn't. Instead, they turned their attention to the bodies of their dead companions, immediately embarking on a further feeding frenzy - all except Dark Eyes - its attention was focused on Jack. The creature was practically standing on its hind legs, defiantly daring him to approach. Jack instinctively strengthened his grip on the wooden length of the scythe, not taking his gaze from Dark Eyes' direction for fear of attack.

Yes, Jack was afraid. He didn't know why but he knew his plan had gone horrifyingly wrong. Having had to claw, bite, and slash at the living moving flesh of their siblings, having to watch and listen to their pitiful cries and struggles, it had *changed* them, turned them into something macabrely different.

Jack knew he'd unleashed something demonic in their nature of which nothing good could come.

*

Within a few weeks, there were markedly fewer rats about the farm as evidenced by the apparent reduction in rat droppings. To Jack and Sarah, it was becoming a case of *out of sight, out of mind.* Jack felt quietly pleased with himself, believing the fear he'd experienced had been brought on by the surreal sight of the rats tearing and feeding on the torn flesh of their dead companions.

But it was a sight he'd be reminded of time and time again over the coming months.

*

The county had enjoyed quite a respite from its rat problem, but for Jack and his neighbours, there were signs of its return. Rat droppings around the farm were even higher than before the barn incident. The occasional sight of a lone rat darting across a yard had increased to several sightings a day of three or four at a time.

Sarah was complaining of seeing even more of them scurrying about now - but not *like* before; they were no longer running for the nearest bolt hole at the sight of a human or one of the dogs. Their numbers increased until they were confident enough not to scurry away at all, slowing their agile stealth to more of an arrogant stroll. Most disturbing was the sheer variety of rats, all mixing, the bigger brown rats and the smaller black ones, and every shade of colour in-between roaming together in huge packs.

Jack tried to rationalise it as some unexplained spike in the rats' breeding cycle - that's what his neighbours thought, why shouldn't they? Jack, on the other hand, he could easily have answered that last question. But he didn't want to admit to himself or his neighbours that he was probably responsible, not only for the 'spike' but for something worse to come …

The rat problem was not getting any better, and Jack was at his wits' end. His fear of the worst-case scenario being Sarah or one of the kids suffering a single rat bite had escalated to fearing for their very lives.

Several neighbouring farms were reporting seeing large numbers of rats swarming across their land, and more recently, garbled stories of attacks on livestock. Initially, Jack had tried to dismiss them as nothing more than the cider-fuelled ramblings of a lot of old codgers.

"I tell ya's all again," the grizzled old farmer, Pete Myers, was saying from his usual place at the bar in the village pub, "they're getting out of control, and sommat's got t'be done I tell ya."

A few of the locals were listening intently, rolling their eyes, and nodding their agreement while Old Pete retold the story of his mutilated half-eaten sheep: "Was like nothing I ever saw I tell ya, torn t'shreds it was but not like how you'd expect it t'look if some dog'd done it. No, it was bloodied all over, like a thousand little claws and teeth had been scratching and biting away at it over a long time, and then there were all them rat droppings around it. What more proof d'yer need than that I ask ya?"

Jack had listened carefully to Old Pete's gory ramblings, still hoping things weren't as bad as the old boy was making out. He chose not to add to the discussion, knowing if he admitted his fears and told them *all* about Dark Eyes it would put him right at the centre of the problem.

Jack didn't have to wait long before being reminded of the urgency and genuine danger of the situation. The next day, Jack was finishing his midday meal back at the farmhouse when Sarah answered a knock at the door by their postman, Bill:

"Come on in. Jack's in the kitchen having a bite to eat so go straight through."

Bill nodded, skipping the usual pleasantries and social chit-chat …

"Hello, Jack. Is there somewhere we can speak. *Privately* like?" Bill asked, lowering his voice so's not to be overheard by Sarah who was pottering about outside.

"Sure. Come through to the sitting room."

"I found your dog, Rufus, a few feet off the roadside on my way back to the village, just beyond that far-side field of yours the other side of the stream."

"Found him? What do you mean, is he hurt or …?"

"He's dead, Jack. I can't describe it, but it's another attack like the one Old Pete was raving on about in the pub last night. I didn't have anything I could carry him in, and really, you need to come and see for yourself."

Bill hadn't exaggerated. Jack felt sick to his stomach at the sight of the family dog. It had been a vicious attack. The flesh and innards had been ripped out and stripped to the bone. Little else was left of the Bull-Terrier cross's body apart from some skin and fur hanging off the skeleton.

It did look as if Rufus had put up one hell of a fight though, Jack thought, judging from the twenty or so torn and battered dead rats scattered within a few feet of where Bill had found the poor dog.

Were it not for everything that was going on and the usual rat droppings near the scant remains of Rufus's body, Jack would have wondered what could have done such a thing. To have torn a muscular, healthy dog to shreds like that it would have been easy to put it down to some escaped wild animal from a zoo. But Jack already knew what it was.

It had not been his intention to tell Sarah about Rufus at all but to quietly bury the dog away from the farm somewhere. Instead, he brought him back, and once their two young children were safely tucked up in bed, threw the mutilated remains across the kitchen table for her to see - perhaps now she would finally see sense and take herself and the kids to her sisters as he'd pleaded weeks ago, Jack hoped.

"Do you see now, Sarah? That's what I'm talking about. You have to take the kids away before something worse happens!" Jack screamed at her.

"Or would you prefer to wait until it's John or Lizzie lying there instead of Rufus?" he added just to emphasise the point.

She packed the things they'd need that very night.

*

Many of the locals were seriously considering selling up. More and more 'Farm for Sale' signs were springing up every day. Jack decided he'd be adding his own to the list as soon as the estate agents opened again on the Monday after the weekend.

That Monday never came for Jack. In his anger and frustration, amplified by the half bottle of Scotch he'd downed, Jack had started blasting away at any and every rat he saw.

A shotgun was hardly the most practical weapon for killing rats, but the ones he hit were blown into a thousand bits, sending their flesh and blood in as many directions.

Dark Eyes himself had nearly fallen victim to the drunken Jack's alcohol-fuelled rage. A random shot had shattered a window frame of one of the outbuildings in which Dark Eyes and many other rats had taken refuge from the harsh weather.

The blast from the shotgun had sent large fragments of shattered glass and wood flying everywhere; several had lodged in many of the rat's bodies, killing some and injuring many more.

The rats reverted to their natural behaviours, running to whatever hiding places they could find, anywhere away from the blast range of Jack's shotgun. If Jack had been thinking straight at the time, he would have realised it was his one opportunity to escape while the rats were still confused and panicked by the gunshots. Instead, he chose to lock himself inside to sleep off his drunken stupor.

*

Jack awoke with the hangover from hell. He vaguely remembered having blasted away at some of the outbuildings where he knew more of the rats had settled.

He reached for the phone to call a neighbour but found the land-line had gone dead, and with that, the internet too. He then tried his mobile, desperate to contact someone, anyone who might help, but the severe weather was still interfering with reception.

Jack had heard nothing about any rats on the local TV channels. He wondered if perhaps the radio might have received some calls from someone whose land-line or mobile was still working and hurried to the kitchen where the Roberts Rambler radio was. He was grateful now he'd not given in to Sarah's urging to replace it with a newer DAB model with all the internet radio channels on it.

He fiddled with the tuner to position the radio station slider to one of the local radio stations. To his surprise and horror, there was news.

"... drivers on the B237 have reported having to slow down or even swerve to avoid large swarms of rats ... yes, that's right, that's the word people are using to describe their numbers ... so far there's been no reports of any accidents as such, but the Highways Authority have said they'll despatch patrols to the area to look into it ..."

For the rats to have the numbers and confidence to be openly crossing main roads was not good. Such was the swiftness of their spread across the local area, no one had spotted where the attacks had originated and seemed to radiate out from Jack's farm; Jack had kept a low profile by reporting only enough to be consistent with the experiences of the immediate neighbours. But all that was irrelevant now. Jack knew he had lost the battle for his farm. It was just a question of if he could win the battle for his life.

Jack gazed out of one of the living room windows, assessing whether he could make a run for it. Not a chance, he realised. Hundreds, maybe thousands of the little bastards had descended on the farm, like a guerrilla army abandoning its hit and run tactics to attack openly.

Ideally, it would have been best to jump in his Land Rover and drive as quickly and far away as possible. It was in clear sight, tantalisingly close just twenty yards away out in the yard. He thought about making a run for it, trying to reach the car before the rats brought him down.

He had left it too late. The bastards had chewed and clawed at the heavy-duty off-road tyres until they were little more than so many scraps of torn rubber. The metal rims of the wheels supporting the three-tonne vehicle were already firmly dug into the soft ground.

Seeing his only possible means of escape sabotaged, Jack knew he wasn't going anywhere anytime soon.

They were all around now, biting, scratching, clawing at every barricade designed to keep them out, and not just from the outside. He could hear them under the floorboards in those few parts of the house where wood and other more modern building methods and materials had been used instead of the more traditional stone for the area.

Jack was sure they were following his every move and footstep, inside the partitioned walls of the interior of the stone-built farmhouse. The cellars too had already fallen to their onslaught, now filled with dozens, if not hundreds of them - perhaps thousands more were waiting in reserve right outside for all Jack knew. He was close to panic mode, imagining now every worst-case scenario his mind could conjure.

The sound of the rats in the basement and foundations was getting louder and louder. He wanted to take refuge upstairs to put some distance between himself and the noise of below. Again, he'd left things too late; those same scratching noises that filled the air downstairs were being echoed in the roof.

A violent thunderstorm had been raging for the past hour, pelting the farmhouse with heavy rain, driving ever more of the creatures to seek refuge inside the farm buildings.

The rats had trapped Jack in his own home more effectively than he'd ever managed to snare any of them in his rat-killing traps.

The sound of the rain hitting the roof had effectively masked the noise of their activities, but the smaller black roof rats had returned and made themselves a cosy home in the attic area immediately above. Most of them had disappeared from the main living areas following their temporary reduction in numbers a few months back. That had been a real bonus, especially for Sarah who despite a more tolerant attitude, was still loath to sharing a home with them. But now they were back, having multiplied at least ten-fold since the beginning of the storm. Jack desperately regretted the disastrous idea to try setting the rats against each other. More were climbing into the attic and roof spaces with each passing minute.

The slightly larger brown rats, of which Dark Eyes was a particularly vile and gruesome prime specimen, were natural burrowers. They quickly dug their way beneath and into the foundations of most buildings, especially rural farms like Jack's, and were making frightening progress. The sturdy traditional stone structure was, for now, preventing the rats from breaking through the farmhouse defences and barricades, but he knew they would eventually find a way in.

The electric lights flickered and then went out. It was still early evening but being February, the daylight was already fading. With the thick storm clouds overhead, Jack knew he'd soon be in near darkness. All he could do was wait for the inevitable now.

Jack's and the neighbouring farms and villages would be just the beginning.

*

No sooner had the first one managed to gnaw through one of the small areas of the floorboards and the heavy wooden planks Jack had nailed down over them, he knew it was over. Soon they would be scrambling through every little opening they could find.

Within minutes, hundreds more swarmed the room, dragging him to the floor. He made a token effort to fight them off. It was futile. Surprisingly though, once he was down, they paused in their biting and attack. He lay there motionless, that is until he saw Dark Eyes crawl up onto his chest. Not so surprisingly, that was the moment Jack lost control of his bowels and bladder. The rats barely seemed to notice.

Dark Eyes remembered what the two-legs had done to them in the barn, forcing them to tear the flesh from each other to live. The hate-filled rat looked again into the two-legs' eyes. Jack looked back. This time he was the one having to look up. Dark Eyes was again standing on its hind legs from his position on Jack's bloodied chest.

With a twitch of its tail, it was the sign to Dark Eyes' rat soldier army to resume their feast of the two-legs' flesh. It was fortunate Jack was the only human on the farm. The scream that briefly escaped his mouth before a thousand rat bites tore and shredded his throat was a sound no human being would ever have been able to forget

*

A month later, Dark Eyes' attention was caught by the sight and smell of the bare skin of all the new two-legs going about their business. Many had turned up at the abandoned farmhouse in their moving metal boxes for reasons beyond the rat's understanding.

The army had arrived and called a state of emergency. But Dark Eyes welcomed their arrival. The warm blood and soft, tender flesh of the many new two-legs would nourish all the new and future little ones in the days, months, and indeed years to come.

Scavenging among the discarded left-overs of the human two-legs for food was a thing of the past. The two-legs wouldn't just be providing the rats' food … they would *become* it.

***

Old Max

Old Max was as mighty and vicious a brute of a dog as you could find. Tom Selby had conditioned the old mutt through a brutal regime of punishment and reward. In truth, Old Max never saw much of the latter. Tom Selby's idea of rewarding Old Max was just to ease up a little on the punishment.

Tom Selby worked and exploited the old dog in any way he saw fit, and if that included earning a few extra coins on the dog fighting circuit so much the better.

Old Max had growled and bared his teeth at any and every provocation as a pup before Tom had broken his spirit. There was only so many times his small young body could take the full force of a leather whip cutting through his fur and skin. And when that didn't work, it would be a hard leather boot kicked into his side.

Old Max was too smart not to realise that strength and ferocity alone wouldn't ever put an end to his suffering. The ageing dog had long since learned to heel at his Master's command, or to at least play the part of the obedient 'man's best friend.'

It was inevitable that some of that cruelty would rub off on him despite once being the gentlest most adorable looking little pup there ever was, the sort that could melt a stone heart quicker than the morning sun melting a snowflake. But that cute little bundle of furry joy was gone. In its place stood a wretched hate-filled creature from hell. Instead of being cute and adorable, he had a look to rival that of Cerberus, the three-headed crazed canine Hound of Hades guarding the gates of Hell. And just as any man or creature alike approaching his mythical counterpart, anything that still breathed coming near Old Max would be greeted with a snarl, a growl, and flash of rabid drool dripping teeth. Bitter experience had taught Old Max never to show his back to a stranger for fear of what might land across it.

*

Old Max was having a long and lazy snooze in the sun, a rare pleasure he'd been lucky enough to enjoy while his Master was suffering a bout of influenza; there was no loyal vigil by his Master's door or bedside.

Far from pining for Tom Selby's return to health, Old Max would gleefully have torn into the man's throat, ripping fat and muscle from the bone before joyfully bathing in his Master's blood like a playful puppy splashing and jumping in a mud-filled puddle. Old Max had no such happy puppy memories.

Still half dazed from his sleep, this was a rare unguarded moment for Old Max. He could feel something small and warm beside him. Fur and little whiskers were gently tickling him, not that it was unpleasant in any way, quite the opposite. But it was equally rare, if ever, for Old Max to allow another living creature to come so near.

Mixing with other animals usually meant being pitted against some new opponent in the dog fighting pits when his Master needed money for his debts.

Old Max was curious though. He looked down at the small furry ball-shaped mass, asleep and blissfully nestled into his tummy. Old Max's natural instinct was to spring to his feet and rend the little creature limb from limb to satisfy his hunger. It was a constant hunger that came from a lack of food other than the few meagre scraps his Master saw fit to throw him from time to time.

For whatever reason though, Old Max didn't stir, content to allow the little furry mass to continue its equally contented slumber.

A little later he was again awoken by the small bundle beside his tummy. This time it wasn't the gentle tickling of fur and whiskers that had stirred

Old Max from his sleep. The small warm mass, apparently now an infant rat to a fully awake Old Max, was shivering and half-starved, trying to snuggle the old dog's body for extra warmth. Despite his hunger, Old Max reached for one of the tiny meat scraps lying in his feeding bowl and dropped it near the infant rat's mouth before starting to lick at its body. The warmth of his tongue and the copious amount of drool soon warmed the little rodent body.

The little rat had stirred a protective instinct in Old Max; he shifted his position to cosset the rat's body in a thicker and longer part of his own fur.

*

They say all good things come to an end, and so it was for Old Max when his Master recovered from his influenza. Those three short weeks had been the happiest time of Old Max's life – no beatings, no dog fighting pits, and no fear.

Old Max knew he wouldn't survive many more fights - he was still as brave and ferocious as he ever was but the daily beatings and accumulated battle injuries were taking their toll, as was the passage of time. Old Max was indeed becoming 'Old' - each new opponent in the pits seemed just a little younger and stronger while Old Max was equally just a little older and weaker with each additional fight.

*

Tom Selby had debts that needed paying. He looked towards Old Max. It had been three months since their last visit to the dog fighting pits, more than long enough for the old mutt to have recovered. He'd heard that a newcomer in one of the neighbouring villages had a couple of tough young rottweilers he was desperate to arrange matches for. He'd also heard they were the most vicious dogs anyone had seen in years. No one was that keen to risk theirs against them. That might be to his advantage though, Tom Selby thought; he could demand a bigger share of the purse, and if Old Max should manage to win one last time, it'd make him an even more valuable asset for a few more fights in the future.

*

Little Whiskers hissed and spat his anger at the enormous two-legged creature that was dragging Old Max by some cord around his neck. Old Max was obviously reluctant to accompany his Master to wherever it was they were going.

The tiny rat had never seen a human up close until now. He wasn't impressed - they smelt and looked funny, and they didn't appear to have any proper teeth or claws.

He wondered why Old Max didn't just turn and sink his fangs into the soft exposed flesh of the two-legged creature's neck - surely it couldn't be a match for Old Max's strength and teeth or be able to resist a swipe from one of Old Max's massive paws with his claw-like nails outstretched. Little Whiskers wasn't to know – he had not yet witnessed the two-legs' cruelty and cowardice of which they were capable.

Without warning, Tom struck Old Max across the back and side with a riding crop. Little whiskers was startled by the whining yelp that practically exploded from Old Max's mouth. The force of the blow drained Old Max of his strength, almost causing the old mutt to buckle under his own weight.

Again, Little whiskers hissed at Tom Selby, and this time several more of his friends emerged from various hidey-holes to dart in and out of the lumbering human's path. The shock at seeing so many rats about his feet startled him. He dropped the leash he was holding Old Max by and stumbled back. Spotting the separation between Tom and Old Max, Little Whiskers ran between them, urging Old Max to follow in the direction of the adjacent barn.

Together they made their escape from Tom Selby's sight, disappearing inside the barn. It was a welcome respite to Old Max being able to slump into the soft, warm hay to soothe the still smarting lash of the riding crop. He wondered if he'd done the right thing though, following his little friend into the barn? Tom Selby's use of the riding crop on Old Max was the first real cruelty his little friend had yet seen of any human. He knew his Master wouldn't let a few rats prevent him from dragging him back on their journey to the dog fighting pits. There was no doubt the delay would mean further cruelty along the way.

Sure enough, Tom Selby appeared in the doorway to the barn. He towered over both Little whiskers and Old Max, and all the other rats darting back and forth at his feet. Tom gave an angry kick with his foot that sent a few of them tumbling away in a rolling motion to the side. He then grabbed hold of Old Max's leash and tied it to one of the support beams before grabbing the nearest implement, an old heavy manure shovel.

Little Whiskers leapt at the two-legs' feet, trying to bite at the ankle area, but the farmer's leather boots were too high and thick for the little rat's teeth to penetrate. Tom Selby took a step back and swung out at the creature.

The force of the shovel sent the little rat flying several feet into the air before landing in some loose hay at the far end of the barn. Old Max barked and growled his anger at the way his only ever real friend had been set upon by his Master. Old Max strained at the rope around his neck, the hated leash keeping him from springing to the little rat's defence. He would gladly have endured any amount of pain to tear free from whatever it was he was tied. For the moment though, even Old Max's great strength and determination weren't up to breaking the grain of a two-foot thick solid oak support beam.

Where brute strength was insufficient, stealth and guile and a thousand little razor-sharp teeth were doing better. The latter was busily gnawing away at the individual threads of the rope leash. In its half-chewed and weakened state, it wasn't long before it gave way to one last determined tug from Old Max, catapulting the old dog up at his hated Master. Tom Selby instinctively raised his arms and hands to protect himself, but the sheer weight of Old Max hitting him head on sent Tom crashing to the ground. He tried desperately to shield his face from Old Max's snapping jaws. The cruelly treated dog responded by sinking his fangs deeper into his Master's forearm flesh.

Old Max was revelling in an inexplicable frenzied joy, and the opportunity to at last tear flesh and muscle from the bones of his Master, happy for his fur becoming soaked in the hated Master's blood.

It would be no easy task though - Tom Selby was a big man, and a strong one too, strong enough to put up quite a fight against a dog in the twilight of its years. But Old Max wasn't fighting alone. Little Whiskers and a hundred or so of his kind had amassed round Tom Selby's body on the ground, each nipping away at the clothing and succulent flesh beneath. Hundreds of vicious bites and scratches stabbed at the farmer's body from what seemed a thousand different angles and directions. Tom's high-pitched screams practically assaulted Old Max's acute canine hearing. They were the last sounds Tom Selby would ever make.

*

Tom Selby had lived alone on his farm and wasn't the sort of man who attracted many visitors.

It was nearly a week later when a neighbouring farmer, Jim Franklin, called at Tom's place to collect on some debts. It looked deserted but for the wretched unattended farm animals. Jim recognised a farm that had been neglected in its daily tasks for several days at least.

He did a thorough search of the house and outbuildings, expecting to find Tom either drunk or hurt.

Jim eventually found him in the barn. He saw straight away Tom was dead.

He thought at first that Tom must have injured himself and discarded some torn clothing among the blood-soaked hay judging just how little was left of the body once the rats had had their fill of it.

It had been Old Max's larger teeth and nails that had inflicted the injuries and bleeding that led to a quicker death than Tom Selby deserved.

Little Whiskers and his kind hadn't been too bothered by that. They were as content feeding on a dead body as they were feeding on his live one.

Like most farmers and other country folks, Jim Franklin was no stranger to seeing the devoured remains of a dead body, just not one almost picked to the bone, even less so a human one. He could see from all the rat droppings nearby what had done this. Had it not been for that, he would have thought the vultures had been at it for several days.

Jim's attention was distracted by the sight of Old Max appearing in the doorway to the barn, but what held his attention was the sight of Little Whiskers by his side. It was a surreal sight, this massive brute of a dog with this tiny rat nestled alongside one of its front legs. The little rat was seemingly unafraid under the protective wing of its canine friend. Jim smiled.

He had a soft spot of Old Max and had always resented Tom Selby's treatment of him.

Old Max slowly approached him, his teeth discreetly hidden from sight as were Little whiskers,' trotting alongside. Old Max was acutely sensitive to the nature of any given human but knew this familiar one to be friendly.

Jim fell to one knee and held out the remains of a half-eaten sandwich to Old Max before dropping a small part of the offering to the ground for the wee rat too. Both accepted the gesture and fed on their unexpected meal.

"Well Old fella, you fancy a new home with me?" Jim asked, gently stroking the back of the ageing dog's neck. Neither Old Max nor Little whiskers understood the words, but the soft, kindly tone was enough to entice Old Max into following Jim to his horse and cart, and to a new home and life in the twilight of his years.

Just before jumping into the back of the cart, Old Max stopped and looked back to where his little rodent friend was still standing. Little whiskers stood on its hind legs and looked back at them. Little Whiskers knew Old Max's proper place was with a human Master, one that would love and care for him. The two-legs who had fed them seemed like such a one. What the little rat didn't know was what its own place was. Rats and the two-legs were hardly natural friends - would the two-legs want it tagging along?

Old Max looked up at Jim with a tearful glint in those wide brown eyes before turning to look back at his little friend, torn between the two.

Jim could see warmth and gentleness in Old Max. They were qualities Old Max had hidden almost all the time he had been with the now very much deceased Tom Selby. Jim could also see loyalty in Old Max, devotion to the little creature that had befriended him in some way Jim would probably never know or understand.

Again, he fell to one knee and patted the front of his thigh, beckoning the little rat to come and join them.

In the years that followed, Jim Franklin was oddly enough the only farmer for miles around to never have a problem with rats on his farm.

***

A Ghostly Terror

Jacobs Manor had an unusual array of occupants even before its latest arrivals to the family, all long since dead of course. Like many a country house, it had its fair share of wildlife lurking in the cellars, the walls, and every other nook and cranny where nature's smallest and darkest creatures take refuge: spiders, mice, cockroaches, and of course the usual complement of rats scurrying about its dark corners. It had been many years though since it had any human occupants in residence, at least not living ones.

The ghostly residents looked on with eager curiosity as the removal van pulled up outside the main entrance. They had suspected for a while they might be getting new arrivals with all the recent building and renovation work that had been going on. For the most part, they had let the workmen go about their business unhindered.

Specialising as they did in renovating such places, the builders were all past being troubled by the occasional wailing, creaking floorboards, or harmless apparitions that were an integral part of these old houses, especially ones with a history to rival of that of Jacobs Manor. Nonetheless, they had sworn they would never set foot in the place again for any future work. They weren't sure if the old manor was genuinely haunted or just infested with stubborn vermin. It didn't matter how many rats they got rid of with the usual traps and poisons, a couple of times when their work had carried on into the early evening, several of them had reported seeing a small spectral like creature. Some even claimed it would scurry across their path, sometimes leaping at them, seemingly from thin air. But work was work, and so they had kept their fears and sightings quiet from the manor's new owners.

*

It was good having humans living there again. The presence of warm breathing living flesh seemed to inject new ghostly vitality into the manor's spectral occupants. It was never their wish to scare or harass their living housemates, and so most humans got used to them. All except the rat that was. The rat hated living humans and was none too fond of its fellow spectres either; the rat took as much delight in scaring and tormenting them as it did any human dwellers of the manor. While the dead were immune to any human interference, they were vulnerable to those of their own kind. The rat horrified them much the same way a living rat repulses living humans. What made it worse, there was no way of killing or getting rid of it the way the living dealt with their own vermin. For centuries, both they and living occupants of the manor had had to put up with the spite-driven vengeful ghostly rat ... several of the latter had literally been terrified to death at the sight of gleaming white teeth and claws hovering about their face at all hours of the night. It was those that the rat now shared the manor with, in the same unearthly spectral realm.

*

The Earl of Dewsbury, the original owner and builder of the Manor back in the 16th century had been a practitioner of the sciences and black arts as well being a brutal sadist. Had he been born in modern times, psychologists would have earmarked the Earl a future serial killer with his liking for tormenting small animals. One of his victims had been a little black rat. The Earl had caught it and several others in one of his trapping cages. The contrast of its jet-black fur and almost fluorescent white teeth gave it a chillingly demonic look which fascinated the Earl. He noticed too the jet-black rat had killed the other occupants in the cage to live off their flesh. This exceptional rat harboured a savagery to match his own. The Earl's vivid imagination and fascination with the black arts led him to wonder if indeed some demon possessed the rat ... he was determined to know. What followed was all sorts of experimentation the Earl believed to be sophisticated science and black magic. It was mostly nonsense, but amid all the potions and spells, the Earl had unwittingly trapped the rat in that spectral realm between the living and the dead. It was not a place meant for animal souls except those who were so intertwined with their human master's they couldn't be separated. But that's where the rat found itself, not that it was complaining; it knew it would never die in the way others of its kind did after just a few years. It had learnt too to enjoy and even revel in the endless torment it could inflict on both the ghostly and the living alike. And so it went on down the centuries. It dismayed the other spectres of the manor the number of living the ghostly rat had driven from what could have been a lovely stately home for them all, enjoying peaceful co-existence. They hoped it might be different this time, that the rat had wearied of its spiteful nature and would allow the humans to live in peace with them.

The rat had also watched the new arrivals with interest. It was especially pleasing to see they had a cat. If there was one thing the rat hated more than anything, alive or dead, it was cats. It remembered several past experiences from when it was alive. The rat shuddered at how they had toyed with it in their playful 'cat and mouse' games, almost killing it several times with their fur and skin ripping claws when cornered.

Bill and Louise, the young couple who had bought and renovated the manor had brought Bill's mother to live them. She was a sweet old lady and would make a fantastic babysitter for the child they were expecting. She was also devoted to looking after the family cat, Molly. The two were inseparable ...

"That's right, Molly, you come and sit on mummy's lap," the old lady urged the ageing cat. Molly purred and nestled into her usual comfy position. Her mistress gently rocked in her chair, stroking the generous amount of fur the cat still possessed despite the frequent moulting in its twilight years.

Seeing the lavish care and love the human was doting on the mangy looking flea-ridden cat was even more reason to hate it, the rat decided. And the old human too. It was going to take immense pleasure in tormenting them both, knowing it was safe from the earthly harm it had once been vulnerable to from such wretched creatures. And then it would turn its attention to the other two humans.

Molly was busy amusing herself chasing the many little mice and even some of the rats that made a home of the old disused cellar areas of the manor. She was of little danger to them now that she was no longer as agile as she once was. Still, it was in her nature to play the part of the hunter even if all her food did come from the very best suppliers before being lovingly prepared by her mistress.

It was during this latest 'cat and mouse' game the ghostly rat made its first appearance. It had shrieked its unearthly hiss in Molly's ear just before appearing to leap across her path. Molly had been startled by it and instinctively swiped her paw at the apparition. She was delighted to see she had caught it full on only to be instantly disappointed for the rat to vanish. Time and time again, the ghostly rat would appear and disappear into thin air, leaving the sound of its high-pitched shrieks ringing in her ears. Molly was getting on, and the rat was easily nimble enough to avoid her but seemed to delight in showing off just how invulnerable it was to Molly's attacks. It was a constant annoyance that its body was impervious to her swiping paws. There were times when Molly could hardly contain her frustration, seeing her claws harmlessly pass through the rat's spectral form. It was like the rat was playing its own 'rat and cat' game with her instead of the other way around.

The rat decided it had enough of tormenting Molly directly, knowing it would distress the creature even more by turning its attention to her mistress instead. Night after night the rat would hover above the old lady's face, knowing that its fang-like teeth would be the first thing she saw when waking up. It had only taken a few such sightings to reduce her to a tearful nervous wreck.

Not wanting to worry her son and daughter-in-law, especially not in her 'condition,' the old lady hadn't told them about the waking nightmares she was having. Molly knew of course. She had seen the rat hovering above her beloved mistress, powerless to help or protect the old lady. The ageing cat was slowly growing to hate that spiteful, vicious little rat; ordinarily, she would only tease and play with such creatures, but this one, she would have gladly torn it to shreds if only her claws had something substantial they could tear into.

A month had gone by and the old lady had resorted to taking tranquillisers and medication to sleep as often as she could, anything to shield her from the rat's appearances. The rat was patient though. It would watch for hours at a time, waiting for the exact moment the sleeping pills wore off, hoping to catch the old lady while in that dreamy state between slumber and consciousness.

It was all too much for her, and so she died. A sudden and massive heart attack had sent the old lady 'to her final peace' as the doctor had put it, trying to cushion the blow to Bill and Louise, still blissfully unaware of its other residents.

It was heart-breaking for them that she hadn't lived just a little longer. They knew how much she had wanted to hold her first grandchild, but it wasn't to be … and nor was there to be any 'final peace' if the rat had its way …

Molly was desolate at the loss of her mistress, rarely moving from beside the bed in which she had slept. So depressed was Molly, she was even indifferent to the rat resuming its tormenting appearances, much to the other creature's annoyance.

Bill and Louise tried to care for Molly the best they could, knowing the cat was too old to survive long if she didn't eat or drink something. Three days later, Molly died. The vet assured them that there was nothing more they could have done for Molly, how it was not uncommon for a pet to die soon after the passing of a beloved owner.

The ghostly rat was pleased to have dispatched the two of them so soon following their arrival at the manor. It was even more pleased when it sensed the old lady's returning as the newest spectral resident of the Jacobs Manor. She wasn't there yet but was getting ever closer, slowly drifting her way to the other side of life's curtain; it would then have all eternity to plague her for long as it amused the human-hating little rat.

Night-time was descending, and Jacobs Manor's resident ghostly rat was looking forward to again tormenting the now dead cat-loving human the closer she got to their spectral realm. The rat knew she would be at her most vulnerable when she arrived, confused and afraid while coming to terms with her new state of existence.

The old lady crossed that curtain, first to the room in which she had died, and in which she had last held her beloved Molly. The rat lay in wait, ready to pounce once again – it wasn't just the living that could be terrified by such appearances.

The old lady started to appear, gently swaying in her rocking chair. The rat was confused at how serene she looked, like she was content - it was not the fearful and unhappy state in which most humans crossed over, the rat observed. No matter though, the rat decided as it prepared to make its presence known again, readying itself to leap out at her.

The rat never made that leap. It was Molly instead who leapt from the old lady's lap. She too had 'crossed over' with her beloved owner, and now with all the speed and vitality of her youth. That was why the old lady hadn't looked afraid or confused as the rat had expected. She had her beloved Molly back. And this time, the cat *was* able to protect her mistress. This time her retracted spectral claws *were* able to rip through the rat's body, splattering the floors and walls with the ectoplasm equivalent of the rat's blood. It couldn't kill the rat, of course, it was already dead, they both were. But this inability to die was something the vicious little rat would regret for all the days Molly chose to hunt and torment it.

Molly remembered the rat's spiteful nature while she was alive. It was the rat that had frightened her mistress to death.

In life, Molly's greatest joy, apart from basking in the old lady's attention, had been the playful and gentle teasing of tiny animals, though rodents of any kind were her favourite. She was looking forward to enjoying that pleasure once more. But it wouldn't be the gentle, playful teasing of before, not with the ghostly one that had plagued them both in their final days … she had all eternity to indeed hunt and inflict vengeance on her mistress's ghostly terror.

*

Bill and Louise were to live long and happy lives in the manor. The 'other' residents too were at last free of the rat's torments, not that it had gone. It was as much trapped within the walls and grounds of Jacobs Manor as they all were, but it was a better place now. The manor's only remaining rat problem was of the warm flesh breathing kind, and one they could safely leave to their living human residents to deal with.

The tormentor had now become the tormented, spending all its time and energy trying to elude and escape Molly's nightly hunting of it. It wondered how many centuries' more suffering it would endure at the claw clad paws of the creature that had once been its victim?

***

Cute Little Pets

Despite most two-legs' revulsion of them, some are very fond of rats. A few even choose to keep rats as pets, looking after them the same way they care for and love their cats and dogs. Such rats are lucky indeed.

Most though are forced to live quite miserable lives, having to fight and scavenge for food from the two-legs' filthy left-overs. And when the two-legs aren't attacking them, they still have to watch out for the body-crushing traps and the bad food that makes them die.

Another danger is the great metal boxes the two-legs sometimes move in; if a rat wasn't careful, such a 'box' could kill a rat in an instant if it hit or ran over a rat.

Worst of all are the horrible underground tunnels where most are forced to live amid all the two-legs' droppings. It seems the only places safe from the two-legs and their traps also happen to be the filthiest and most dangerous in other ways. So yes, those rats lucky enough to be cared for as pets are practically the royalty of the rodent world.

*

An elderly couple, Geoff and Emily Jackson, were two such two-legs who kept rats as pets. They bred them too for others who also saw the beauty in the little creatures.

The Jacksons had a large detached house with a vast overgrown garden on the outskirts of the city. It was an absolute paradise for all the Jacksons' pets.

The rats that had been born there quite innocently thought this was a normal life for them, unaware of the not so nice reality of the city, or even just beyond the security of the house and garden walls that enclosed them.

Geoff and Emily were returning from a shopping trip when they caught sight of what looked like an overgrown mouse lying to the side of the road. They assumed it was probably dead but stopped just to make sure. Neither would have wanted it on their conscience had it still been alive and they had done nothing to help.

They had been right to stop. The mousey brown coloured creature was weak and exhausted, probably from lack of food the Jacksons thought, but it was still breathing. They picked it up and took the tiny bundle home with them.

"Poor thing," Emily said, placing the little rat on the examination table, "it looks half starved."

"Well, let's see what we can do for the little chap. Hopefully, we'll have it up and running about in no time," Geoff answered her.

They were both trained veterinarians, albeit long retired now, but still well able to treat the little creature. A closer inspection at the roadside had already revealed it to be an unusually small rat rather than an extra large mouse. They had both laughed at their original assumption; it was this mistake and the creature's mousey brown colour that prompted them to call it Mousey.

They took a few blood and saliva samples to check it wasn't carrying any disease or infection that might be passed to their other rats.

It would not be long before they were sure of the results, but in the meantime, they kept it separated from their other patients and pets. It was clear from just looking at it, this was a wild or city rat, hardly suitable to sell as a pet.

Once they had fed and watered it, Mousey thrived, and they were delighted to learn the mousey brown coloured rat was disease free. Not only that, but it was now recovered and healthy too after just a few days care.

It seemed a remarkably curious and intelligent rat. Its eyes followed you wherever you went, watching what you were doing. Both these qualities made it ideal for adding to their current breeding stock. Yes, the Jacksons were pleased to have found this unusual little rat.

One universal trait Mousey did share though was that it was a randy little bugger. Three weeks later, the young doe it had been 'placed' with gave birth to a healthy litter of rittens. Emily and Geoff were thrilled with the look and quality of the new arrivals, knowing that each would make an excellent and loving companion for someone.

In the days that followed, the Jacksons continued to notice their newly recovered rat's curiosity about them, about everything really. But something was wrong. They saw too the many times Mousey would just stare out of the window, or scurry around the perimeters of their garden wall like it was looking for a means of escape.

Despite the care and comfort these two-legs could offer, Mousey was pining for the freedom it had always known.

The other rats had told it that there was no such escape, but were curious why it would want such a thing? They had an enjoyable and comfortable life here, especially in comparison to the awful life Mousey had described. They had been horrified when they learnt of the dangers facing others of their kind beyond the safety of the only home they had ever known. They could hardly believe it about the traps that could slice a rat's body in two, or even imagine the filth and smell of the cold, damp sewers where most rats had to live.

Hard to believe too was what else the new rat told them about most of the two-legs beyond their idyllic life with the Jacksons, of their hatred for rats, and of leaving poisoned food for them. The *very* worst though was about *themselves* – how they would attack and kill members of their own mischief that were diseased or injured, and even cannibalism during famine or overcrowding. The stories the city rat told instilled in them a new appreciation of the life they enjoyed.

A few weeks later something happened to disturb the tranquillity of the Jacksons' lives and their menagerie. The opulence and relative seclusion of their house had attracted the attention of three escaped prisoners from a remote prison a few days before. The escaped felons had done well to get so far in such a short time, but if they were to stay free, they knew they had to rest up somewhere. They figured the Jacksons' house would make for a suitable place to hide. They needed food and money too, and again, the house looked a safe bet for both.

Late that night, all three men climbed the garden

wall. They lowered themselves down a rope the other side to lessen any noise they might make than if they simply dropped the twelve-foot height. Upon reaching the ground, it was easy to make their way through the cover of the overgrown garden to the main house. Mousy watched their approach. Of all the rats and small animals that had free roam of it, only Mousey had much experience of the two-legged creatures beyond that of Geoff and Emily Jackson. Mousey's instincts told it these two were up to no good. Why else would they be arriving in the dead of night, through the cover of the garden to the back entrance of the house? Mousey didn't understand of course about hiding from the authorities or the need for money, but it still suspected these two were doing what every rat had an inbuilt skill for – scavenging.

The three men were hoping to find food and shelter, and whatever else they might find useful for their survival. That alone would not have bothered Mousy; all creatures did what they needed to survive. But it knew the two-legged scavengers were far more dangerous than their rodent counterparts; they would not just take what they needed but would kill and take everything they could. And these were clearly prime healthy specimens. Mousey feared the frail and elderly Geoff and Emily would be no match for these other two-legs' youth and strength.

The alarms and other superficial deterrents had

been simple enough for the three skilled criminals to by-pass with ease. They were now in the house, making a cursory appraisal of its contents. From what little it had seen of them, Mousey judged the two-legs to be skilled scavengers, and probably worse. Mousey knew it probably didn't have the time or indeed the means to gain entry to Geoff and Emily's room to somehow alert them to the danger. The other rats had opted to follow Mousey's lead in whatever must be done.

At Mousey's direction, some twenty rats scurried about the two-legs' feet, darting in and out in all directions. The two-legs were startled, and like most of their kind, repulsed at the sight of the rats, clearly visible in the light of the moon illuminating them.

"What the f...?" one of the men shouted, kicking one away from his foot.

"Uh? Rats, fucking hundreds of 'em," a second of them cried, his horror of the filthy vile creatures echoed by the third.

In the heat and confusion of the moment, each of the two-legs had temporarily forgotten their need for quiet before realising they might have woken the occupants of the house in one of the upstairs bedrooms. One of them rushed to search for where the elderly couple were. The last thing they wanted was for either of them to phone for help. It was a big house though, and they were on the far side of it. Mousey had hoped the two-legs would have made much more noise, enough to wake Geoff and Emily in time to call other two-legs to their aid. But Geoff and Emily remained asleep in their bedroom. The two-legs had soon discovered the Jacksons' bedroom and woke the elderly couple, threatening to kill them if they tried to resist or made too much noise.

Geoff nodded that he understood, looking at his wife to do the same. For the moment, it looked like Geoff and Emily would be okay so long as they cooperated with the escaped prisoners. Mousey suspected otherwise; these two-legs were just biding their time before they killed the old couple.

"We need money, cash-card pin numbers, anything you have. Give us what we want, and you'll be okay," one of the two-legs had said to Geoff. Mousey didn't understand the words, but their tone was clear. It was threatening, as was their body language. Everything about them was bad.

Despite the seriousness of the situation, the rat saw little else it could do for the two-legs that had nursed it back to health. Apart from what could only be described as cute little pets, Mousey wished it had more of its natural brethren to attack the two-legged enemy, aggressive survival driven rats from the streets rather than these tame genteel ones.

In the previous few days, Mousey had managed to gnaw away at the one small area of thick wooden fencing to the front of the house. At least the rats would have a means of escape. But even with Mousey's assurances that life as a wild or urban rat could be a good one, the others opted to remain with their elderly carers, even if it meant dying with them.

Mousey understood their decision. They had no instinct or skills for any other kind of life. These tame rats had done well to scare the two-legs the way they had, but they had no idea about survival. The learning of skills like biting, killing, and scavenging in the way of their wild and urban cousins was not high on the list of attributes that made for a cute little pet.

They had much to learn and little time to do so …

Two days passed. Geoff and Emily remained alive. The escaped prisoners knew they could kill the defenceless couple anytime they wanted, but for now it made sense not to. By holding a knife to the throat of either of them, they could be sure the other wouldn't do or say anything to arouse suspicion in the event of any the couple's friends or neighbours calling.

The three humans were enjoying their time at the Jacksons' house. They had plenty of food, it was warm and comfortable, and they were safe from prying eyes or nosey questions. Apart from the occasional business call, it was clear the Jacksons kept themselves to themselves. From the relative seclusion of the house, one of the two-legs was going back and forth to a local cashpoint, slowly draining the Jacksons' bank account.

Another week would be enough to clean out the last of the Jacksons' savings and be moving on, the two-legged trio thought.

Though Mousey had no concept of time the way the two-legs did, it vaguely knew a few more risings and settings of the great warm yellow light might be enough.

Despite their pleadings, the Jacksons had not been allowed to attend to the care of their rats. Oddly enough this suited Mousey; it had hastened the return of the 'pet' rats' natural hunting and survival instincts. Without the Jacksons providing them with their lovingly prepared meals each day, most of the rats had not been averse to scavenging through the kitchen bins and garbage bags of the two-legs. A few though were taking their lead from Mousey and feeding off their smaller rodent cousins among the garden dwelling field mice. Each passing day had seen the cute little pets revert ever further towards the creatures they were born to be. They had learnt to hunt and kill their prey … and what's more … *they were enjoying it.*

Mousey could see the two-legged intruders were becoming more aggressive with the old ones of their kind. The little rat knew the time was close when no doubt the two-legged intruders would kill Geoff and Emily before leaving for new scavenging and hunting grounds. But his new friends had surprised him; they may have lived a privileged and sheltered life until now, but they had been quick learners in the ways of their wild and urban cousins. And with their selective breeding and generous, healthy diet the Jacksons had provided, these pet rats were bigger and stronger than most of their kind, certainly more so than Mousey. They didn't yet have the wile and cunning of the likes of Mousey, but they were every bit as capable now of sinking their incisors deep into a two-legs' throat. Mousey was proud of their transformation.

*

"I'm so scared, Geoff. The rats must be terrified, and so hungry too, that's if they haven't died by now? If only they would let us feed them, see if they're okay?"

"I know, I know," Geoff was saying in reply, holding his wife close to give the reassurance she so desperately needed. He was so proud of her, worrying about their pets.

It was clear to Geoff that his darling wife didn't fully understand their own danger, something he was glad of. He thought it best not to share his fears that only a miracle was likely to see them survive their ordeal.

*

The three two-legged intruders had been drinking heavily that night. In fact, they had been overdoing the beer and whiskey for the past several days and nights. Mousey knew the signs; it was making them even more dangerous and unpredictable. But Mousey saw advantage in it too – the strange liquid the two-legs liked to drink also made them slow. Sometimes it made them stumble and fall too. If nothing else, it deepened the sleep they would fall into, making them less alert, more vulnerable …

"We should make this our last night here," the leader of the three escapees was telling the other two, "we've been lucky so far, but we've got all we need from them now, and sooner or later the old couple's disappearance will be noticed."

"Agreed. We leave tomorrow then?"

"Yes. We'll kill them in the morning, I'm too fucked to be doing with all that tonight."

The third one of the trio had already passed out on the living room sofa and had been left there to sleep it off. From the safety of one of the bookcase shelves, Mousey watched the other two stagger their way upstairs to their room. Had the escaped two-legs been less drunk they would surely have heard the rustling and scratching of some twenty more rats from behind various sections of the skirting board, each waiting to act on Mousey's cue.

An hour or so passed and there was no further sound to be heard of the two-legs stumbling in the dark upstairs. The one on the sofa was breathing heavily, its chest gently rising and falling. Pig-like snorting sounds were expelled from its mouth, but otherwise, it remained quite still. It was a warm night, and the two-legs was wearing just shorts and a t-shirt he had taken from Geoff's clothing. It left much of its flesh exposed

The rats emerged silently from several small holes they had previously gnawed in several areas of skirting board obscured by the Jacksons' furniture. Mousey was already perched on the arm of the sofa, looking down at the two-legs' face just a foot or so away, its whiskers twitching in anticipation of the bloodbath to follow. Two more rats were looking down from the top of the backrest. A few of the others had sidled up beside the two-legs' torso while a couple more were nestled alongside its crotch area. Mousey gave a quiet screech. That was the cue for the two higher up on the backrest to leap down at the two-legs' throat, landing but a fraction of a second after Mousey had landed on its face, ripping away at the two-legs' eyes. The other two rats did likewise with the throat; their hunting of the garden living field mice stood them in good stead – they didn't hesitate when sinking their teeth into the soft, warm flesh, clawing at the surrounding tissue at the same time. The two-legs tried to scream but the only sound to be heard was a sort of gurgling as blood started to fill its throat. At the same time, it felt a searing pain elsewhere about its body. Several rats were tearing away at the tendons around the two-legs' ankles. The two-legs tried to jump up but only succeeded in slumping off the sofa, hitting the floor with a thump. More rats set about its body, striking from all directions. Even Mousey was surprised at the sheer viciousness of the attack, but amid their natural instincts, these now not so tame rats remembered this was one of the two-legs that had terrorised their beloved carer. It was going to pay, and not even Mousey was able to stop them indulging in a bloody orgy of mutilation.

Another hour passed, and life had now deserted the two-legs' body, as had most of its blood. Mousey twitched his indication that they should proceed upwards towards where the other two-legs were hopefully still sleeping. One by one they scurried after Mousey. It was like a scene straight out of a horror movie, this moving carpet of fur and glistening teeth ascending the stairs like a trickle of water flowing uphill. When they reached the room the two-legs were sleeping in, their progress was temporarily halted by the closed door. It was to make no difference. Mousey's newly trained army had been busy in the proceeding days and nights, having gnawed away access to the different rooms … no part of the house was now barred to them.

Since both the remaining two-legs were in the same room, the rats' task would be more difficult this time. Had the rats been double or preferably triple their number, Mousey was sure they could have killed their enemy with ease. As it was, with just over twenty, their attack numbers for each of the two-legs was reduced to a mere ten. There was a danger that the two-legs' combined defence might be enough to ward off the rats if they split their numbers evenly between their bigger two-legged enemy. Better to concentrate most of their number on just the one. Meanwhile, Mousey intended that it and the same two rats that had leapt at the other two-legged one's throat would launch a more precise and targeted attack at the two-legged intruders' leader.

Like their now dead companion downstairs had been, both the two-legs were sleeping soundly. The one Mousey believed to be their leader was in a single bed while the other was sprawled out on a sort of long couch, much like the sofa downstairs. Both were making the variety of noises Mousey had come to associate with sleeping two-legs, notably those worse the wear for drink. Mousey had seen and smelt many such drunken two-legs on the streets of the city, and even in some of the sewer tunnels.

Mousey along with two more of his friends, the same two that had so efficiently helped rend the very life from the other two-legs, stealthily got into their respective assault positions. Mousey would again go for the eyes while his two larger companions went for either side of the two-legs' throat. Mousey was relying on the remaining rats to overwhelm the other two-legs by sheer weight of numbers and multiple assaults like before. They wouldn't have the street-wise city rat leading them this time, but their previous attack would give them confidence and the thirst for similar bloody success.

Mousey and the two 'lieutenant' rats for the attack on the two-legged leader were but inches from the targets of their teeth and claws. The other rats were also in position to leap at the other two-legged enemy from all sides, including the eyes and throat just as Mousey had demonstrated before. Like so many coiled springs, each rat awaited their cue from Mousey. But for the breathing of the two-legs, the room was in complete silence, and darkness too. With their poor eyesight, the darkness made little difference to the rats; they could more than compensate for it with their other senses and the sensitivity of their whiskers that aided them in their movement and navigation much like bats relied on echoes.

It was essential that neither of the two-legs should be able to come to the aid of the other. Both attacks were to be simultaneous ... they waited ...

Mousey screeched the command to begin the assaults just before landing on the two-legs' face. It was unfortunate for the little rat that the two-legs chose that precise instant to shift its sleeping position; instead of biting and sinking its teeth directly into a nice juicy eyeball, the little rat had been thrown slightly off target and was only able to dig a claw into one instead. At that same exact moment, one of the two lieutenant rats sunk its sharpened incisors deep into the gently pulsating artery running along the two-legs' neck. Had it not been for the sudden and unexpected movement, it would have been an even deeper bite in the heart of its throat.

The second of the two lieutenant rats also had its attack disrupted by the two-legs' movement and had to make do with randomly slashing and clawing the side of its face. Nonetheless, the rat left strips of skin hanging from the two-legs' cheeks, accompanied by a thick and flowing stream of blood. This time though, their victim was able to rise to its feet despite the ferocity of the attack. First, his upper torso had practically catapulted itself into an upright position when the rats first struck. Instinctively the two-legs swung its hand to dislodge the rat from its face. In doing so though, it flung Mousey away while its claw was still embedded in one of its eyes. In propelling the little rat away, the little rat also tore the said eyeball from its socket. The two-legs screamed the sort of scream you imagine to be reserved for the very depths of hell. It was hard to conceive just what kind of pain could induce such a sound, but combined with shock and panic, it was a sound that no two-legs or rat could ever forget once heard.

Though Mousey wasn't to know it at the time, its fellow rats in the other attack were having more success. There weren't as many of them as Mousey would have preferred but still enough to have quickly brought unimaginable pain to another of the two-legs that had upset their previously happy lives. Each had indeed managed to bury every injury inflicting millimetre of their natural nature-given weapons in the throats and both eyes of the target. The rats swarmed over the writhing body that had rolled over and hit the floor. At first the biting, scratching, and clawing was limited to the exposed parts of the two-legs' flesh. The rats wanted more. Soon they were ripping away the thin layers of clothing, revealing further areas to gorge themselves on.

The two-legs' life was fast slipping away even if the strength and loudness of its screams might have suggested otherwise. So busy were most of the rats feasting on the still living flesh, it was only the piercing scream of the other two-legs that momentarily distracted them. A few of them scrambled in different directions to avoid being trampled by the other two-legs' hurtling through their number before diving headlong through the bedroom window.

There were bushes and long thick grass surrounding most of the house. Most of the ground was quite soft too, so it seemed unlikely that the fall would have been fatal. It hardly mattered though. It was severely injured, and now half blind. Its companions were already dead, and it was unlikely in its injured state it would be able to threaten the Jacksons to help it further – the danger was passed.

Mousey and his army of pet rats scurried to the room where Geoff and Emily had been locked. The piercing screams of the two-legs when one of its eyes was ripped out and during its jump through the window had obviously woken them. They had assumed the escaped prisoners to be fighting among themselves and opted not to call out to ask what was happening; Geoff and Emily hoped they would be forgotten about or not thought worth bothering with if the men were fighting. They held each other close, fearful that their time might have come.

Mousey and some of the other rats were busily gnawing away at the foot of the door to the Jacksons' room. Several more had entered the room via the many secret passageways they had created by gnawing through sections of skirting board into the spaces in the walls. The Jacksons looked down in stark amazement, watching as several of their pets scurried past their feet to gnaw away at their side of the door. Emily wanted to scoop them up in her arms, but Geoff urged her not to.

On both sides, the rats concentrated on the lower door-hinge area. Once their combined gnawing efforts had all but destroyed the support function of the lower door hinge, the sturdy oak door creaked and strained to support its own weight. Enough of a gap now existed for more of the rats to swarm under the gnawed part of the wood. Again, the Jacksons looked on, astonished and bewildered. The rats continued their teeth and claws assault on the wooden door and doorframe. Geoff realised what the rats were doing and took the initiative …

"What? What are you doing, Geoff? We were told to stay away from the door."

"I don't think they're still here, my darling. We've not heard any sound since that scream, and no one's come to investigate the rats at our door. Trust me, darling."

Geoff put his shoulder to the door and pushed. He was old and frail, but he was a big man. His weight added to the weakened state of the door was all that was needed to send it crashing down. All the rats had now amassed about the Jacksons' feet. A few had joined Emily on the bed where she was sitting to watch what was going on. The touch of warmth from the rats reassured Emily. The scene of them nestling beside her somehow told Geoff too the miracle he had hoped for had somehow come to pass … their ordeal was over …

*

Epilogue.

DNA and dental records identified the two bodies in the Jacksons' house as two of the men the police were searching for – there wasn't enough left of them for facial recognition. The sight of the mutilated bodies had initially shocked the Jacksons. To Geoff's surprise though, Emily had proved quite resilient during the immediate aftermath. These were after all the same men that had been prepared to allow her beloved pets to starve. She would lose little sleep over their deaths, quietly hoping the escaped one would meet a similar end too someday.

Mousey took the opportunity to quietly be on its way. The unusual little rat liked the Jacksons. They were the only 'good' two-legs it had ever met, but Mousey was born to a different life. Some of the other rats were torn between enjoying the freedom that loomed before them, and not wanting to desert their beloved two-legged carers. Most opted to remain. Perhaps Mousey would return one day to see how they were doing – its freedom to do so was at the heart of its decision to leave. It never was and never could be any two-legs' *cute little pet* ….

***

Ratcula

It was fascinating to watch so many of you gripped by your own fear and panic, not knowing if or when you or any of your litter might be next. That was nearly 700 years ago, back when even I was young, barely a century past my time as a ritten. Since then I've killed and turned more of your kind than you will ever know, but then, of course, I've had time on my side.

You see, I am immortal - an immortal rat to be precise. My mortal kin rarely live more than two or three of your years so imagine if you will how truly old that makes me.

Most humans find it difficult to believe me. Are you all so arrogant as to think the beasts and demons you fear are exclusively large and two-legged? Let me tell you, dear humans, we immortal monsters exist in every size, shape, and form.

I sometimes wonder if the 'Old One' of your kind that made me the way I am ever considered what being immortal would mean to a rat? I say 'your' kind, but that's not strictly true, for indeed, he's more akin to mine now - you may share the same number of legs, but we share the thirst, a thirst for the blood of all your kind.

The Master, the one who turned me, he lived across the great river, way south across the land to Transylvania. I was little more than a ritten the first time I saw him, with but the finest covering of wispy black hair and only the tiniest sight of teeth and claw to me. But having few of the weapons I would need to hunt and scavenge for food didn't mean I didn't have the hunger for it.

The Master's manservant was skilled at training creatures in the art of hunting and killing my kind. He had more than a dozen ferrets for invading our tunnels and secret spaces or for digging and burrowing into the soft ground where we birthed our rittens in the lowest reaches of the castle. They would pursue us into whatever recesses in the earth we could find before forcing us out for the dogs to rend us limb from limb.

And both had been doing their job well of late then. It had been by chance alone I had escaped their latest campaign to rid the castle of us. It was something they could never do, but for now, it had left me the only survivor of my litter, and without food.

The whereabouts of the manservant's or Master's food stores were unknown to me. I wasn't to know the Master of the castle didn't eat in the way mortal creatures do.

I was still unskilled in the ways of scavenging, with only my primordial hunting instinct to rely on. Over the coming weeks, I did as good a job as any of the ferrets at ridding the castle of its remaining population of mice. I had become as skilled a hunter as any of my older kin had been before the dogs got them. And that was to determine my fate - having hunted my little mammalian food source cousins to extinction I was facing starvation again. I still had to stay away from the manservant for fear of his dogs and ferrets nearby, just leaving the living quarters of the Master himself.

It was as well we were both nocturnal creatures for I never saw him during daylight hours when he would disappear for over twelve hours at a time, though he was almost as rare a sight even after the setting of the light from the sky.

I never saw his manservant bring him food nor the Master visit the kitchens. I assumed he must have food in his room. I looked about it as best I could, not having the means or intellect to open locked cabinets or pull open drawers. When I found nothing, I gnawed holes in them, such was my hunger, but still I found nothing. I knew he must eat sometime. I would follow him where he went that night before the light of the sky came back.

I was surprised when I found myself following

him deep into the cold, damp bowels of the castle, deeper even than I had ventured for I had never thought there might be food there. Again I followed, more out of curiosity than hunger now as I could still not see or smell any food. The Master came to a door at the bottom of some stone steps, each one ground down into a hollow from what I now know to be the weight of his nightly pacing down them over the past thousand years, from long before the castle above had ever been built.

He had closed the door before I could follow him into that room. I searched for and found another entrance, a small narrow tunnel some way along the wall, no doubt dug by others of my kind. I entered it, wondering what I would find on the other side.

There was no sign of the Master, just a large box. It was a grand box, thick solid oak, ornately decorated but still just a box, the sort you humans like to use to bury your dead.

Still being an ordinary mortal rat, I had no concept that that must be where the Master was. Perhaps there was food in the box though? There didn't appear to be any opening or way of looking inside. It was good that it lay directly on the ground, meaning I could more easily gnaw my way inside. There was no food in there though, just the Master lying in it - The Master's body was as cold as the room's stone floor.

Young though I was, I knew the difference between a living body and a dead one. My instincts told me this one had not had the warmth of life in it in a long time even though it was but an hour before I had seen the Master walk into the room.

All this was too much for my instinct-driven rat mind to fully comprehend and once again my hunger for food became my only focus. The other two-legs had held the Master in awe, and even the dogs and ferrets seemed to recoil in terror in his presence as I would for reasons I did not yet understand. Now though he was just a lifeless body, one that hadn't rotted and returned to the earth, one that could still sustain me for many days and nights. With no other food in sight, I resolved to eat of the Master's dead body.

I opened my jaws the widest I could and plunged my teeth through the material of his clothing, my teeth sinking deep into his flesh beneath. The softness of it surprised me given it was dead. And even though it was icy cold, blood flowed from it like it would from a live body.

Still being an ordinary mortal rat, I had neither intellect nor understanding, but my primitive instincts were screaming at me just how wrong this was, how wrong it all was. I suddenly became afraid, again for reasons I still had no understanding. It was only my burning hunger that stopped me from scurrying away faster than if all the manservant's dogs and ferrets were chasing me. Without warning, the strangest feeling ran through my body as I swallowed that first morsel of cold dead flesh, the icy cold but still flowing blood wetting the sides of my throat. My stomach seemed to explode from the inside, making me completely forget my hunger.

The dead body I had just started to feast on leapt to its feet, sending the lid of the box hurtling upwards and across the stone dungeon-like room. I would have run, but an indescribable pain was coursing through every part of my body, totally paralysing me.

The Master reached down and grabbed me, his fingers and thumb firmly gripped about the entire girth of my body, his grip breaking my ribs, crushing my insides. It was not just his strength squeezing the breath from me, but his shortly trimmed nails had grown into claws, easily piercing deep beneath my fur and skin. He held me up almost at arm's length. It was impossible to believe, but the Master's teeth were as long and sharp as any of my own kind, or any of the creatures of the woods. How this was made no sense to me; I knew the humans had neither teeth nor claws of the kind to defend or attack, or so I had been taught - but *I* was wrong - *all* my kind were wrong.

With his teeth fully bared to me, I could see the angry fire in the Master's eyes blazing brighter than the burning logs in the fire grates that warmed many of the castle rooms.

I knew at that moment my time had come, that I would surely die as the Master brought me towards his face before biting into my body. I was still in pain from the dead flesh and blood I had already swallowed from the Master's body but the agony that followed, even after near on 800 years, the memory haunts me, my fur and whiskers bristling whenever I think of it.

The wailing squeal my crushed lungs produced grew in intensity until it turned into a roaring scream; were I human, it would have been the equivalent of a bellowing volcano.

The Master tossed my limp and almost lifeless body to the stone ground. I felt the dark and nothingness of sleep overwhelming me, probably for the last time, I believed.

*

"Hello, little rat," I heard a voice saying to me. It was the Master's voice I heard. I was still alive. How could that be?

"You'll be hungry I imagine. There's food in the bowl for you," I heard him add. I didn't understand, or rather, *I did understand.*

We had heard the humans speak, of course, understood the tones and loudness of the sounds they made, even recognised a sort of meaning in a few of them. This was different – I *truly* understood the Master's words, both in sense as well as tone or any of the other subtleties of language. He knew I was hungry and was telling me there was food immediately to hand in the wooden bowl that lay a few feet away to my side. I didn't know *how* I knew that, but I *knew.*

And he was right. I was hungry, hungrier than I had ever been in my life. It was a different sort of hunger though - not the empty stomach kind but more like a cross between an insatiable thirst and a desperate need to breathe.

I turned towards the bowl, descending on it with a speed that surprised me. The smell of the food was overpowering, the unmistakable scent of fresh blood. I plunged my face into it, lapping it up as like it was to be my last. I continued drinking the red nectar till it was gone, and even when there was no more to be had I licked at the rough wooden bowl, determined to devour every minuscule drop clinging in the grain of the wood.

"Feel better now?" The Master asked. Again, I understood. But how to answer?

"You can't speak, not as I do, little rat," the Master answered, knowingly:

"But you don't need words, not with me, not with anyone. Without human vocal cords to make proper sounds, the turning and the thirst have given you the gift of speaking with your mind, what the humans call telepathy, a gift they lost long before even *I* was first born."

A whole new world of understanding had opened up to me. 800 hundred years later and I still have no words that can describe what it was like awakening that night - not just being blind and waking up sighted but as one never having ever known that others could see.

I understood words, language, meaning. I could look about me and know what things were - a table, a door, a bookcase - things that had been obstacles or just something to scurry and hide behind till now. But I still had questions, *many* questions …

"What's happened to me? How did this happen, what does it all mean?"

As the Master had said, I couldn't make the *sounds* of language like he and the humans could, but I could articulate words in my mind, and I knew he understood. I had already deduced that the Master was not like other humans, perhaps not human at all?

"I don't know, not exactly. It was when you bit into me and swallowed some of my blood. It did something to you. Not enough to turn you, not completely, but something half-way between."

"I still don't understand? Turned? The thirst? Half-way?"

"By drinking of my blood, you acquired my immortality and the thirst for fresh living blood to live but without the strength and speed or the telepathy that allows you to communicate. I sensed it in you when I picked you up. I was angry with you; I was tempted to leave you as you were. It would have been a miserable life, possessing the desperate thirst for blood but not the intelligence to understand it, not having the strength to overcome your natural enemies, having to feed off the smallest and vilest of creatures without knowing why."

"But you did something to me? I do understand. And I feel strong, and … so much more."

"Yes, I did. It would have been wrong to leave you as you were. You weren't to know what I was; you were just a hungry animal acting on instinct. Instead of biting you it would have been a mercy to have devoured you whole when I grabbed you up from the ground."

"But you didn't. Something when you bit me, it

made me stronger, made me more - *like you?*"

"Yes. When I bit you, I only took a small amount of blood while allowing my saliva to enter your bloodstream. That's what completed the turning, making you what you are now."

We spoke for many hours after that, through the night almost to the rising of the sun, an event he explained he was forever barred from seeing. Sunlight was lethal to him, the Master told me.

"And what about me?" I asked, "will sunlight kill me too?" Already my newly acquired understanding was taking hold. It was no longer the mysterious yellow light from the sky, it was the sun.

"No, it will not," the Master answered, "you have a gift of which I'm immensely jealous. Smaller blood creatures like you are for reasons I've never been able to discover, immune to the sun's blood boiling effects on such as myself. The strange warmth of it won't kill you as it would me, but neither will you be as strong or as fast during the day, you will be more vulnerable."

I might not have cared were it not for the fact the poor eyesight we rats possessed was now as sharp as my teeth since the turning, ideal for a life lived only at night, but I was not to be so restricted.

In the several years that followed, I would accompany the Master on his nightly jaunts to the surrounding towns and villages to feed. Many times I dined on the same human he had chosen, both of us taking only enough to satisfy our thirst. But I was a rat – a predator used to doing its own hunting and feeding, not some tame pet leeching off its owner. The Master understood this and when he felt I was ready, left me to hunt my own food.

I had no wish to feed off other rats, though I would if I had to, but feeding with the Master had given me a taste and thirst for human blood now.

It was not to be as easy as I imagined. I had thought with my new awareness, and speed and strength far exceeding that of my mortal brethren, hunting would be a simple matter.

My minuscule size made it impossible to approach and strike directly at the neck of a human the way the Master did. The human preference for wearing shoes or boots and thick clothing made it equally difficult to strike at ground level most of the time

The females of your kind were more accessible to feed on, leaving their lower legs and calves more exposed beneath their skirts. It was a pity not more of them were to be found or choose from in the late hunting hours. Fortunately, there was rarely any shortage of males after dark, many falling to the ground after a night in the taverns and alehouses. It was easy for me to sidle up beside one to take my fill from an exposed hand or about the neck. My smaller size made it easy for me to fully satisfy my thirst with a relatively small amount of blood. I had to be careful though – sink my teeth too deep and I would pass on the blood craving, a mistake I made several times in those early years. It was not until over a century later I was to discover one of the abominations I had created during one of those early feeding hunts.

With the passing years, I became aware of another thirst, one every bit as strong as the one for blood. I yearned to see more of the world than the tiny one that existed within the walls of the castle and the surrounding countryside. The time was coming for us to go our separate ways …

*

I remember that first day in England when we docked into Plymouth Harbour. I had never dreamed such a place could exist.

It had also been my first time aboard a ship; my Master had brought me aboard to accompany him in his cabin. It was a strange and luxurious way for a rat to travel you might think while most of my kin were scurrying about in the bowels and darkest hidden recesses of the tall sail ship. He claimed it was partly from his guilt for having condemned me to an eternity of bloodthirst as the price of my immortality.

I didn't understand his guilt and regret at the time. The higher intelligence that came with my transformation hadn't yet fully manifested itself. I still had no real comprehension what it would mean to live much beyond my natural lifespan let alone the hundreds or possibly thousands of years to follow.

The journey to England was most exciting, exploring the ship and mixing with other albeit mortal rats. I was immediately aware of their deference. They sensed that I was something more and entirely different …

*

We finally alighted later that night after his current manservant released us from the travelling casket aboard the ship.

I had protested the unnecessary cruelty of the previous manservant in his hunting of my kind. The Master agreed. We both enjoyed several days of fresh warm blood from his successor.

The Master bade me farewell, though not before saying we would meet again someday, and how he looked forward to hearing about my travels. He also warned me never to underestimate the humans' capacity for cruelty and cunning. It was not a warning I needed. I still remembered all too well the dismembering and bloody deaths of my fellow rittens

The Master was right; we were to meet again, each time exchanging tales no human could imagine of our lives down through the centuries, but those stories are for another time. I was still yet to experience my first real adventure.

The master gently placed me upon the stone cobbled streets of Plymouth to begin *that* first adventure.

The presence of so many humans was already making me thirsty. But I had another thirst that needed satisfying too.

My sibling rittens had all been bloodily rent by the claws and fangs of the human trained dogs and ferrets. The gift of self-awareness that came with the thirst had made me aware of another concept – revenge …

It was the year 1347, the year and time your kind refers to as the Plague and the Black Death … they say it was spread by rats?

***

Two Different Specimens

RS2179 had been given its final injection. Perhaps this would be the one to bring it the peace it craved. It hoped so.

It was a cold and clinical reference for a living creature. That was the intention - experience had shown such impersonal referencing to be an effective means of helping insulate the laboratory staff from any guilt. Many a brutal dictator had used similar victim classification systems as part of their extermination processes, mainly when they were short on the sort of person who enjoyed such work.

The tiny creature was number two thousand, one hundred and seventy-nine in the extensive list of rat specimens used in the secret 101 faculty's nasty experiments. 'Secret' was a good description of the place in more ways than one. It was not listed in any public domain. It was purposely hidden away from peer scrutiny, its very existence kept secret from all but the shadowy upper echelons of its parent company. Given what went on there, it was as much a dirty little secret as it was a location.

The little creature sensed it was coming to the end of its relatively short existence. But that was okay. It had not been a good life and RS2179 would be glad to see it over. From the moment of RS2179's birth, the only world it had ever known was the chilly sterile one of the laboratory it had been allocated to. It was never to experience the feel of grass under its feet. The joy of finding some tasty morsel for its next meal was unknown to it. All it knew was the hard, smooth Perspex floor and the dry and tasteless mixture the white-coated laboratory technicians would leave in a tiny bowl at the end of its foot-long cage. The only sounds it heard were the deep bellowing voices of the two-legged white-coats and the hum of the air conditioning unit that kept the experimental environment at a distressingly uncomfortable low temperature. The lack of any other external stimuli seemed to amplify whatever distress the lifeless prison inflicted on those creatures unfortunate to find themselves there.

Within hours of RS2179's arrival a few months before, the experiments had begun. It was a rare day when it hadn't been roughly manhandled from its cage for some new horror at the sharp end of the shiny spikes they would plunge into its body. It had tried struggling and even biting its handlers, but the clothing they wore was too thick to penetrate. The shiny spikes though, they were razor sharp, far more so than its own teeth. And oh, how they hurt. It was a blessing when the rat would sometimes be sent into sleeping darkness less than a minute after one of them pierced its skin. Each time it had hoped not to awaken, only to face disappointment when consciousness returned.

The last few times that had been the worse. Usually, the skin piercing spikes would be stabbed into some rear part of its body. The latest ones though had been directed towards the areas around its forehead. For some reason, it wasn't so frightening when the entry point was out of sight, but seeing the sharp, gleaming tip coming into focus distressed RS2179 so much more.

Unbeknown to RS2179, the laboratory staff had been pumping all sorts of cognitive enhancers into its brain, And, equally unbeknown to the laboratory staff, they were working immeasurably better than their maze running tests would suggest. The microscopic chemical and electrical information exchanges between the synapses were now jumping across time and space, reaching farther out with each new injection.

For now, that wasn't much of a consolation to RS2179. Its use was at an end other than what details might be gleaned from a post-mortem of their effects on its general physiology. That would have been fine were the rat actually dead.

Just as lethal injections were far from being a failsafe procedure with humans, they were even less so with rats. There had been no check on the complete absence of brain activity in the rat, just a rudimentary investigation of its heartbeat and non-response to being gently stabbed at with a pencil. Most of the life had indeed slipped from its body, but deep inside the rats's brain and mind there was still a dying flicker of life, enough to make it aware of everything going on. It had been robbed of its ability to struggle or resist but sadly, not its feeling and consciousness. It was aware of being lifted and placed in the dissecting tray. Then the cold feel of the Nitrile gloved fingers moving about its body, poking and pulling, feeling about its abdomen and head, contorting its limbs into unnatural positions.

Its enhanced awareness helped limit the confusion and emotional distress it might otherwise have felt, but it was a double-edged sword – it now had a rudimentary understanding of the various instruments it could see in its limited field of vision, and even some of the human sounds they were making. Glad though it was, knowing it would soon be dead, the suffering it was likely to endure beforehand was ample reason to be afraid.

"I'm ready to proceed," Lance Nelson told his colleagues. They had already prepared the equipment he would need: a dissecting tray and board, scissors, a scalpel, a variety of probes, and several pins.

RS2179 was again manhandled from the dissecting tray to being placed on its back on a wooden board. Its limbs were stretched out in a spread-eagled position and pins inserted, one through the palms of each of its tiny feet, and three more along its tail. The pins were super sharp and thin, and so the pain of their entry was quite momentary. Still, the rat wished for the darkness and death to overcome it, watching the white-coated two-legged giant reach for a scalpel. Lance hesitated for a moment, imagining he saw a flicker of recognition in the creature's eyes. He dismissed it as a trick of the light and proceeded to cut along the surface skin and tissue of the abdomen. No sound emerged from its mouth, but inside its head, RS2179 was screaming, its short-lived enhanced awareness now given over to overwhelming fear and blind panic. Another perpendicular slice of the scalpel, this time a fraction deeper, sent its pain receptors into over-drive, flooding its mind with sensations no creature, sentient or otherwise should ever have to purposely endure. A probe was used to prod at its internal organs, moving them this way and that to check for inflammation and discolouring …

"Everything looks normal. Respiratory, heart and other organs all look intact. Now moving onto the muscle and fatty tissues," the voice was saying. RS2179 didn't understand the words but realised what was about to happen, watching the scalpel move towards one of its limbs. It was all too much for the suffering creature to willingly endure. Its mind was beginning to shut down, severing itself from the torrent of impulses attacking its pain receptors. The pain was still unimaginable, but it was mostly starting to subside. The end was mercifully close, but there was one more ordeal to come, and the worst.

The scalpel disappeared out of sight. The suffering creature soon became aware of its new location though when it felt the pain inflicting instrument slicing through the back of its skull. Its mind filled with an explosion of light and colour as its brain was literally cut in two. Such trauma came as a blessing. There was no more pain, just the dying of its brain cells and the last remnants of its tortured mind. The last flicker of life passed into darkness.

"Nothing much to be learnt here," Lance said, "might as well clean up. Dispose of it will you?"

*

Three months later ...

Lance Nelson felt a buzzing about as head as he got into his car. He wasn't particularly alarmed by it. There was all manner of wildlife about given the proximity to the nearby extensive forest. The high walls and other barriers kept most of it at bay, but even the faculty's state of the art security and remote location wasn't going to keep out the bugs and insects.

TLS1, the first two-legs human specimen of its kind was laid out on the rocky surface of the cave floor. It had amused the rats to choose a classification mocking that of their human counterparts.

TLS1's mind was now stirring as it returned to consciousness. The first things it saw and felt were the various insects and spiders crawling about its body, biting, and feeding off him - it was a far cry from the clean and gleaming sterile environment of the lab but more than adequate to serve the same purpose. The human specimen was in pain too. That was the first realisation that everything about him was horribly real and not the nightmare he had thought, and indeed hoped it might be. There was a thumping in his head, worse than the mother of all hangovers, and he was sure of a couple of cracked ribs too. He could just about roll his eyes to look down and along his body; he was bruised and scratched. Another worry was being naked as he was. How had that come about? Had he been kidnapped? Something to do with his work at the lab he speculated. His mind began to clear. He could see rats, lots of them darting back and forth, just out of reach had he indeed been able to move.

Those same creatures he had once experimented on and cut into pieces now inspired in him the same sort of fear they must have felt.

He was briefly reminded George Orwell's novel, 1984, and the Room 101 scene where people would be confronted with their own worst fears. The central character's overwhelming fear had been rats. It dawned on him why the research centre where he worked was often referred to as the 101 Faculty. Someone's idea of a sick joke? Whatever the reasoning, it was hardly amusing given his present circumstances.

The insects and other crawling things were minute in comparison, and so the rats were content to allow them some tiny share of their spoils. It would have been ungracious not to, especially given the help they had been in delivering the specimen – rats weren't the only creatures being experimented on in 'that' place.

Lance wanted to scream, to struggle, to swat and brush them away just like he would if seeing a fly or a spider buzzing or crawling about his home. None of that was an option now. Not a sound escaped his lips, and except for the occasional involuntary shudder, his body made no response to any mental commands to move. He tried thinking back on how it came to be there. The last thing TLS1 remembered was getting into his car. Something had stung or bitten him. It hadn't been painful, but enough to get his attention. He remembered thinking at the time of being glad he hadn't been driving and paid it no consideration other than to reopen his car door to shoo whatever it was out of the car. After that he'd set off for home, confident that whatever it was had flown off into the night air. And then … nothing.

Like those laboratory victims, this human one had also been rendered incapable of movement or resistance, though not by the same means. The rats had no access to or even the means or understanding yet to administer muscle relaxants or anaesthetising drugs, not that it mattered. They would not have been inclined to using them regardless if they had. They had other means for now, albeit cruder and somewhat less 'humane.'

While still unconscious, several of the rats had nibbled deep into TLS1's naked flesh, not to feed but merely sever vital nerves, paralysing its movement. It was unfortunate for the specimen they hadn't miscalculated and severed more vital ones, either killing or at least neutralising its pain carrying nerve endings too. They had done neither. The specimen remained conscious and aware of the slightest touch to its skin, right up to the gentle breeze of a nearby mosquito fluttering its wings.

The rats' purpose in bringing the specimen there was two-fold. Firstly, they wanted to know just how much tissue loss and damage a human could sustain before death quickly followed. The other reason was a more basic one – revenge; they not only knew of RS2179's ordeal before it died, but they had also felt it too, living every moment of their little cousin's pain and fear, powerless to help. Their minds had been connected, and along with all the pain they had shared, they had also taken on its cognitive enhancements and had their own synapses super-charged. The new-found intelligence it gave them was as much a curse as it was a gift, or so it seemed at the time. It was an experience that would stay with the thousand plus numbered mischief of rats for as long as they lived. It seemed only fair to share that experience with their current specimen …

A lone rat, the dominant one of the mischief, crawled up onto its abdomen. It started to nibble away just above the belly button. Its teeth and claws were more than sufficient to tear away a few inches of skin and the subcutaneous tissue beneath. More of them approached, hesitantly at first. The dominant looked round to them with a nod of acknowledgement. After that, they approached more confidently. The specimen silently shrieked as one it hadn't seen started to crawl up the back of its head and over the face. Claws scraped along its eyes. It tried to close them, the eyelids being the only part of its body other than the eyes themselves that still responded. It was no use. Another rat had joined it, using its claws to pull back the other eyelid while a third used its teeth to literally slice at the eyeball itself. There are no words to adequately describe the sense of panic and revulsion going through the specimen's mind at that moment. And that was just the beginning … it was about to get worse … *much worse.*

The slow and meticulous way the rats tore away at the flesh and internal organs had been calculated to cause the most amount of pain for the maximum amount of time. All the time the specimen clung to life, its blood remained warm and tastier to its insect and arachnid feeders. The rats too were feeding off the extremities, but only in small tiny rat-sized bites. They paid particular attention to its genital area, knowing from its mind the additional psychological impact of that.

*

The rats learnt a lot from TLS1: rates of blood loss, pain tolerances, and even some insight into the working of its mind from their synaptic connection – that last aspect hadn't been as intense or well-defined as with their little cousin, RS2179, but enough for them all to revel in the hated two-legs' suffering.

Despite their giant size and, *for now*, superior intelligence, the two-legs were not so nearly adept at coping with the sort of procedures the rats and other creatures had had to contend with for as long as any of them could remember. The two-legs feared death and would fight its inevitability in any way they could.

They would need more such specimens, different ages, sexes, and the like if they were to learn more. They would also need a more efficient means of getting them too; relying on their insect allies stinging them into darkness was not ideal. The one they had just dissected might well have died in the car crash, and it had been no easy task dragging its body back to their underground cave. As it was, it was already bruised and damaged when they got it. The rats still had much to learn in trapping live prey like the two-legs did, but they would learn from them, adapting their methods to suit their own smaller size and different skill sets.

Still, there remained over a hundred more of the two-legs working at the 101 faculty. There would be plenty of time and opportunity for the rats to improve their skills.

Lance Nelson had taken three days to die. It was a death no creature, sentient or otherwise should ever deliberately have to suffer.

That rats had thought otherwise. Not bad for a first specimen, they congratulated themselves. They could, and *would* do better … *Next time.*

***

The Rat Pits

That great and noble era of Queen Victoria, the age of glory and empire and the march of industry and social reform, or so the more romantic and rose-tinted accounts would have one believe.

It was also the time of our green and pleasant land reaching its most ignoble peaks of cruelty. The early and mid-nineteenth century was as barbaric an era as any; those who enjoyed and partook of the most bestial varieties of blood-sport had any number to choose from.

Virtually every seedy backstreet pub in London and many a country one too offered every cruel and violent vice the mind could imagine. For no more than a shilling, your average Victorian lout could witness a bare-knuckle boxing bout lasting till he watched one man or the other beaten half to death.

For the more discerning, including the Victorian gentry, there were pitched battles between all manner of wild animals, and even fights between rabid dogs and men whose wits had long since deserted them - and never was there any shortage of paying spectators. But one spectacle above all others that excited the Victorian baser instincts was to be found in the infamous Rat Pits, the rat baiting contests.

*

No one particularly liked the Squire, but there was no shortage of sycophants willing to join the entourage of assorted low-life who followed his every word and step.

Squire Saxon hadn't just been born with the proverbial silver spoon in his mouth but more the whole silver service - land, money, and the Saxon name and title - he had them all following his succession to the landed estate he'd so impatiently waited on his father to die.

The Squire's cruelty had started at an early age, burning and pulling the wings and legs off flies and spiders, the sort of odious little child a modern a psychologist would have immediately spotted the early signs of a budding serial killer in the years to come. And they wouldn't have been far wrong, developing as he did a taste for ever crueller and sadistic forms of entertainment.

*

Jack Black was looking forward to meeting Squire Saxon again. His proposal for a Rat Baiting tournament was way more ambitious than any Jack Black seen among the seedier backstreet London Taverns or the ones he and the Squire had organised for the country hunting sets.

"How we doing, Jack, you reckon you'll have enough for my little show next week?" asked the Squire.

"For sure I will. I've trapped loads of the little bastards from round these 'ere very streets," replied the self-appointed King of the Victorian rat catchers, or Jack Black as he was much better known.

"So how be London these days, Jack?" the Squire asked, "my first visit to London, you know."

"Still the same filthy streets for most people, and the houses 'n' palaces just as grand for those born t'better things. Rats've never been too fussed where they infest, be it the Whitechapel sewers or the halls 'n' corridors of Parliament or the Palace, all the same to a rat."

"And not a man alive who knows that better than you, eh Jack?"

"Right enough there, Squire," Jack Black heartily agreed: "I do know my rats if I do say it myself. I got us hundreds of th'nastiest little black as coal dust brutes you ever saw. They're a mite smaller than the browns but these are the most vicious I've bred, and I'm sure they'll infect the others wiv the same hunger. But wiv the browns I got too, we've got several hundred over a thousand rats total for the night. A nice mix O' th'two makes for a scrappier and bloody battle for the dogs, it does."

"I sure hope so, Jack. I've lined me up a couple of the best dogs money can buy just like you said, and they're just itching to go at them."

"I'm sure ya have. It'll be a fine, ferocious battle, no mistake I'm just as sure," Jack Black declared, puffing out his chest in the belief it gave what he said added authority, just like his outrageous clothing.

In all fairness, Jack Black did cut an impressive figure in his flamboyant outfits, usually consisting of a lush green top coat contrasted with a vibrant scarlet waistcoat. Then there'd be the bright coloured breeches with a leather sash inset with cast-iron rats for a buckle - and last, but not least, as tall a top hat as you ever saw.

It was a sight that ensured the Rat Catcher King was instantly recognised wherever he went.

*

The upcoming spectacle was to be the best the city had ever seen if Jack Black and the Squire were to have their way. The vile sport of competitive rat killing or rat baiting as it came to be known, had been mainly restricted to the seedier backstreet pubs. It was a gambling sport in which dog owners would set their dogs in a pit and bet on their dog's ability to catch a fixed number of rats, sometimes by the dozen, in a matter of minutes.

Often the spectators would lay bets on the speed of a dog's rat killing prowess. It was as barbaric and bloody a contest to rival the gladiatorial battles of ancient Rome, with a body count, albeit not human but on a par with many an infamous battlefield. But what Jack Black and the Squire had in mind would take the sport to a new level of gore. The dogs certainly wouldn't be having it all their own way on the night, with a few cruel twists to the usual rat baiting format.

*

Squire Saxon inspected the pits he'd ordered built for the night's cruelty.

He'd decided on bigger, circular ones. These were to ensure the rats couldn't huddle or congregate as they tended to do in the rectangular wire mesh ones found in the yards of most of the smaller pubs. With circular pits, no one place was any safer for a rat than another - there was just nowhere to hide.

Another of his modifications was to have sharp spikes attached to the inner walls of the rat pits, again making it harder for the rats to scurry around the edges at the far reaches of the walls, forcing them to keep venturing farther within range of the dog's snapping jaws.

The last of his custom alterations to the standard rat pit construction was the height of the rat pit walls; rats had been known to leap as high as two and a half feet, so Jack Black had recommended they stick with the customary three feet walls or barriers for the rat pits. The Squire instead insisted they be lowered to just two feet to allow maximum close-up views of the action for those paying a premium for seats looking right into the pits themselves.

Yes indeed, the Squire was looking forward to his night of sadistic cruelty.

*

It was time for the main bout of the night. Squire Saxon proudly boasted of the enormous expense he'd gone to in procuring the services of not only the infamous Royal Rat Catcher, Jack Black, but also none other than the two most celebrated rat baiting dogs in all London and indeed the whole of Victorian England.

Squire Saxon stepped aside to allow Jack Black to earn his fee as a Master of Ceremonies making announcements for rest of the night's entertainments:

"Gentlemen, please, let me introduce the stars of our tournament," Jack began.

"First we have, 'Billy,' the most ferocious 'Bull and Terrier' ever to grace a rat-baiting pit anywhere in the country - 26 lbs of prime pedigree rat baiting sinew and muscle, famous for once having sent over a hundred rats to their deaths inside a shade under 12 minutes. And even more infamous, we have 'Jacko,' a Black and Tan Bull Terrier that even though he's only half the weight at 13 lbs, still holds the incredible all-time world record for rat killing - 100 rats killed in 5 minutes 28 seconds, the equivalent of 1 rat every 3.3 seconds."

Billy and Jacko, though different in size, each had a strong and sturdy build. Both had a ferocious will to fight bigger and stronger opponents or in the case of rats, far greater numbers. Either way, these dogs would fight to their last breath if they had to.

Introductions taken care of, Jack beckoned the two dogs' owners up onto the makeshift stage beside the one of two specially made for the night's rat baiting pits.

Billy and Jacko were valuable and famous dogs, and their owners refused to allow them to be sacrificed in the Squire's tournament no matter how much money he offered. But enough rats were to be supplied for both dogs to set new and bloodier rat killing records.

The two celebrity killing dogs entertained the crowd splendidly, killing over a thousand rats between them to satisfy the sick appetites of the audience. Copious amounts of alcohol, an inbred bloodlust, and urging by the tournament organisers had ensured a frenzied enthusiasm. By the end of the night, new rat killing records had been set, enough to guarantee theirs and the Squire's names another shameful footnote in history.

But the Squire and Jack Black had promised more and bloodier contests to follow.

*

The Staffordshire Bull Terrier was a tough old dog. It had done well to dispatch so many of the wee black rats so quickly, nearly fifty in the first five minutes. Still they kept coming. Each successive wave of the relentless black shadow with its many teeth and claws inflicted countless tiny but painful wounds on the paws and legs of their larger opponent. At first, the rats' task looked a hopeless one in the face of the dog's greater strength and size, but inevitably, one of the rats landed a lucky bite that sank deep into one of the dog's legs. The smell of fresh blood renewed the rats' collective ferocity, signalling the final phase of the cruel contest.

They were slightly smaller than their brown cousins and not quite so strong, but what they lacked in size and strength they more than made up for in speed and aggression. Their smaller size made it difficult for the terrier to sweep down quite so effectively at the rats, with more of them finding space to run beneath his belly and in-between his legs nipping away at them almost at will. Their teeth were too small and ground down for any single bite to have a decisive effect unless they could get right in close as one already had, but cumulatively they were sapping the dog's strength and will. It was experience, a will to survive, and an inherent attacking nature that had ensured the contest had lasted so long. The baying crowd of spectators smelt blood though just as surely as the wee rats did. The dog had taken part in many such battles before, but this time the rats just kept coming, their onslaught seemingly relentless. It didn't understand that's how it was meant to be that particular night. This time the outcome was intended to be different.

Despite the contest starting to turn in favour of the rats, with its hunter origins and aggressive prey-like nature, the feisty Terrier part of the breed, specially bred for killing vermin, it continued the fight, fearless of the rats' greater numbers.

The baying crowd roared and cheered their approval. That was to be expected from the rough and hard drinking lower classes, but their bellowing support was echoed by a fair few numbers of fine gentlemen and their ladies, the esteemed Lord Byron, and the Duke of Wellington among the more distinguished 'guests.'

The final contest had been the most vicious of them all. The brave Staffordshire had fought ferociously before succumbing to the onslaught of greater and greater numbers of rats. The wretched dog lay dying in the centre, surrounded by hundreds upon hundreds of dead and wounded rats.

The referee, an experienced man at such events, was busy ushering the remaining live rats back through the exit doors from the pit. Most were too tired to scurry from his presence. All except for one that was. A lone rat, one of the small black vicious ones Jack Black had referred to was rushing around the pit like some hamster on a wheel. It was almost a comical sight, attracting a few cheers and laughs from the many spectators. And then it stopped, right in front of where the Squire in his very own VIP enclosure overlooking the pit itself. For just a second Squire Saxon and the lone rat's eyes met in a mutual stare.

Squire Saxon was to regret not taking Jack Black's advice and sticking to three feet walls for the rat pits.

The lone rat staring back at the Squire leapt from the pit, probably farther and higher than any man or women there had ever seen a rat jump.

Landing directly in the Squire's lap, the rat was within reach of sinking its teeth into the back of one of one of his hands, which is just what it did in one sweeping lunge.

The Squire jumped to his feet, almost as fast as the rat's lightning strike at his hand, instinctively hurling the loathsome creature back into the pits. He was happy to see it land directly at the referee's feet where it had immediately been slammed with a heavy pitchfork. One of the pitchfork spikes speared the wee rat's neck, eliciting a huge roar from the crowd in the process. No one heard the squealing cry from the wee rat. But *other* rats did, and not just the remaining survivors in the pits.

*

"It's been as a grand a night as I ever had, and I've as much you ta thank as any, Jack," the Squire was saying, and remarkably well given the amount of ale he'd downed.

"Next time I'll be sure ta take yer advice with the pit walls, making 'em higher, like," the Squire added, nursing his sore hand, noticing it was now starting to swell. Had Jack Black been less drunk he would have recognised the symptoms and advised the Squire to seek out a doctor straight away. As it was it was all Jack could do not to fall into the gutters, where no doubt any rats would have tried to ensure sure he stayed.

*

A new breed of rats, no more than a dozen or so, were watching Squire Saxon leaving the Bull and Huntsman Tavern where the night's festivities had come to an end. The largest of them, Long Teeth, for want of a better name for that's what best describes the demonic looking creature, was taking the keenest interest in all the two-legs falling and stumbling out into the night.

Long Teeth and its companions were quite possibly the most hideous rats to have ever lived. The larger and more elongated shape of their heads accommodated far longer fang-like tusks than the natural ground-down teeth of their smaller cousins.

Long Teeth's front incisors were the best part of four inches long, giving it as grotesque and deformed a look you could imagine in a rat, absolute monsters of teeth by rat standards.

These long-teethed rats were unlike any others in the world. Had Jack Black known of them he would have given a year's ill-gotten earnings from his rat baiting and hunting for a breeding pair of these new long-teethed rats. It was as well for him he didn't know of them. *They* knew of him though ...

Long Teeth and its companions continued their surveillance of the Squire. Perhaps it was to compensate for the added grotesqueness of their appearance, but these new creatures were a whole lot smarter too.

The new breed had intended to attack the Squire *En Masse* and then feed off him for a while before leaving the rest of his body for their smaller headed kind. They changed their minds once the scent of infection took hold in his blood and sweat. Immediately they could sense and smell the odour of madness about him, the contamination from that lone rat bite already taking hold in the man. The infected flesh would have tasted much the same, but the disease gave the opportunity for a longer and more insidious form of revenge.

As smart as the two-legs and now as cruel.

*

Hunting and being hunted was the natural order of things. Long Teeth didn't blame the dogs for the deaths of so many of their number. Being more intelligent than the other varieties of rat, it knew the terriers had been bred by humans over generations to hunt them, that it was as much an instinct in them now as for rats to continually reproduce and scavenge.

Humans like Jack Black were the real enemy, the ones who bred the dogs and ferrets for rat killing. When more of their number were born, Long Teeth and the new secret breed of London rats would sooner or later have their day with the hated king of the Rat Catchers. But after the night's activities, the Squire too was an equally hated two-legs.

Long Teeth and his mischief intended him great harm. They wanted the Squire to suffer in proportion to the many that had died that night. It was tempting to attack and sink their many long sharp teeth about his neck. They decided that would be too quick a death.

In the coming days, the Squire's health deteriorated. He suffered terribly from fever and pain throughout his entire body.

A few smiling rats sat perched atop one of the rafters that crossed the Squire's room, keeping a vigil on his deteriorating condition. It was to be a slow and excruciating death, and not one the rats had a mind to mercifully end too soon.

The Squire was mostly left unattended attended by night. When the Squire's nurse was out of sight, the rats would venture down and crawl across the Squire' body.

They would gently scratch at his bared chest - not enough to draw blood or add much to his suffering, at least not physically, but merely to add to the Squire's fear at seeing the sight of a grotesque long-teethed rat staring back at him.

The Squire never did die from the rat bite infection but made a full physical recovery. His mind though, that was something else. The Squire had lain in his sick bed for the best part of six months. Each night the rats would descend from the rafters or out from under the floorboards they'd gnawed through beneath his bed. Some would climb up and sit on his chest and stare into his eyes while the Squire just lay there, fear robbing him of all ability to move. Others would poke their noses under the sweat-soaked sheets before shuffling alongside him in his bed, licking and nibbling away at tiny bits of skin and at the scabs that had formed over the many little cuts and bites.

The rats were always careful not to leave their faeces or urine anywhere near him or any sign that might alert the Squire's two-leg carer to their presence.

Eventually, the Squire's body had fought off the fever. Physically it was a remarkable recovery and a tribute to the care he had received. But there was nothing that could be done to save his mind. *That* had descended into the realms of insanity, realms filled with the memory of rats being torn to shreds by dogs, but always ending with the last memory of watching that one lone rat leaping from behind the circular walls up and onto his hand - and biting it!

*

Such was the sudden onset of madness there had been no choice but to commit Squire Saxon to the Bethlem Royal Hospital, the one that would become better known as the Bedlam asylum for the insane.

He was a big robust, healthy man, so there was no reason to expect his death anytime soon. For the next thirty-seven years, the Squire would daily scream himself hoarse from the memories of that evening attending the rat pits. Several times a night the gentle gnawing at his extremities would raise him from his nightmare-filled sleep, only to be faced with something worse, the image each night of those grotesquely long rat teeth scratching away at his chest or little tiny claws scraping at those same teeth to clean them. Either way, each night the Squire had to lie there, paralysed to resist their nightly torments for the rest of his very long life. There came a time though when finally, tired of the nightly spectacle, one rat decided it was bored of tormenting the now very old two-legs. With a single bite, it's four-inch long teeth were able to scoop one eye and then the other right from out of their sockets before a dozen more joined in a final feeding frenzy of the Squire's body.

It was a well-deserved end.

In memory of the many thousands of innocent creatures that died in the Victorian Rat Pits and all victims of the barbaric blood sports of the time.

***

My Little Friends

Little Terry Stuart couldn't remember when *the man* had put him in the room. He was still too young to have any real concept of time the way an adult had. But it had been a long time ago, long enough for his mum and dad to be really worried about him. He wondered if they still worried, or if they even remembered him now?

Terry could hear a scratching noise coming from somewhere low down. His older brother used to tease him about monsters under the bed, in the closet, and anywhere else from where they might jump out at you. Terry wished his brother was there now. Teasing would be better than what the man - *no* - he tried not to think about that. It was better not to remember what the man did to him, made him do, the man who had locked him in the room and did bad things - *no, it was best not to think about that.*

The little tan coloured rat didn't understand what the two-legs did either, but it knew the smaller younger two-legs didn't like it, that it hurt him, and that it was wrong. It was hard to understand why the two-legs would do things like that to their young. There were lots of things the little tan rat didn't know or like about the older two-legs.

The little tan rat continued to gnaw at the hole in the floorboards beneath Terry's bed to make it easier to squeeze himself through.

The sound of the little boy's sobs when thinking about his family had drowned the scratching sounds the rat's gnawing made, so Terry didn't notice when they stopped. Hungry and tired though, Terry curled up in a foetal position under the single thin blanket the man had left him and fell asleep.

The rat climbed up the bed frame at the end of the little boy's bed. It kept its distance at the far end of the mattress for fear of startling the little two-legs. It was warm and soft so the rat decided to lay in a more comfortable position himself as it looked up at the sleeping two-legs, the moonlight casting a striped shadow across the little boy's face through the barred window.

It was morning, and the light and warmth of the sun on his face woke young Terry. The little rat remained blissfully asleep, also curled up in the rat equivalent of a foetal position.

Instead of being surprised or shocked at the sight of the little sleeping rat at the end of his bed, Terry smiled. It was the first time he had done that in a long time.

Terry got up to pee, and not wanting to disturb

the little animal he gently swung his legs over the side of the bed to get up. There was no toilet in the room, just a washbasin on the opposite wall. For number 'twos' the man had left him a bucket that he kept in a cupboard over at the far side of the room. The man only took it to be emptied whenever he visited the boy to bring him more food and - *other things.*

When he had finished peeing and washed his hands, Terry looked back round at the rat. It was sitting up, looking back at him, scratching at its nose and whiskers the same way you or I might rub our eyes upon first waking up.

Neither Terry nor the rat felt any fear or revulsion at the sight of the other, just innocent curiosity. Terry reached into the drawer of his bedside table. There were still a couple of biscuits in it from the packet the man had left the last time he came. Terry broke off half of one and held it out to the rat.

"*Hello*," Terry silently thought, still holding out half a broken biscuit. The little rat scurried forward on the mattress and started to nibble at the tasty treat the little two-legs had placed down for him.

Seeing how much the rat was enjoying its unexpected meal, Terry placed the other half of the biscuit there for him too while he ate the last one himself.

Terry wondered what he should call his new friend, now that he'd decided the rat was a friend, and all friends had to have a name. He was unlikely to say the name aloud, not having uttered a word since the man had 'visited' him that first time, but he could still 'think' the name.

He was going to call it Bill, but not knowing much about rats he didn't know if it was a boy rat or a girl rat, decided it should be a name for a boy *or* a girl. He called it Whiskers.

With just his underpants to wear and a sheet he used to wrap himself in for clothes, Terry climbed back on the bed and pulled the blanket back over him.

Now that Whiskers knew the little two-legs was friendly it scurried up and nestled beside him, allowing the little two-legs to stroke the back of its head.

Over the next few days, Whiskers came to visit the little two-legs every day, and each day Terry would share what little food he had left from what the man had left him, just crackers, some slices of bread and even a few bits of fruit. Terry never knew exactly when the man would visit again, so he ate sparingly, but Whiskers was only little, so he was happy to share what he had, even when Whiskers started to take some of what he gave him back through the hole in the floorboards under the bed.

Several other rats had also taken to visiting the little two-legs. Terry would smile and even laugh a little while watching the comic antics of his little friends scurrying back and forth before disappearing in and out of the several new holes they had gnawed in the skirting board behind the cupboard.

Terry had long run out of biscuits to give the rats, but he offered to share the last of his other food. Surprising to him, the rats stopped accepting it after the first few days. He worried maybe it was because he had upset them in some way and would repeatedly hold out bits of bread or fruit to them. He didn't know the rats knew he had very little food left to feed himself and were busy exploring the rest of the derelict building for other sources of food that they might bring to their new two-legged friend.

Terry had lost all track of time over the past few months so he was never sure exactly how long it was between seeing the man but it was probably about a week after meeting Whiskers for the first time when the man made another visit.

Terry could hear the slow *thud thud thud* of the massive lumbering bulk of the man climbing the outside stairs leading up to his room. He still had the welts and was sore from the man taking his belt to him last time so knew better than to make a fuss or protest at what he knew was going to happen. There was nothing Terry could to stop the man and so just cowered at the far-side of the room, farthest from the door. He knew, of course, the man would drag him back onto the bed, it was more an instinctive reaction trying to put as much distance between them for however brief a time.

Whiskers and several dozens more of its kind had also been aware of the man's approach, somewhat before the noise of him climbing the stairs from when he first entered through a hidden side entrance.

Whiskers wanted to attack the man as soon as he stepped inside the building but not enough of the other rats had joined him yet for an effective attack. It was for the best though as it made sense for them to allow the man to unlock the door to the young two-legs' room - it was a thick, heavy oak door, and it was doubtful if the rats could have gnawed a hole tall or big enough for the boy to escape through.

Terry became panicked at seeing so many rats. Dozens had suddenly appeared from the many extra holes they had gnawed in the skirting board and around the room and through the floorboards beneath his bed. It wasn't the rats he was scared off though, they were all his friends, but he was worried *for* them; Terry knew there was nothing he could do to protect them or himself, and so desperately tried to shoo them back.

They darted to and fro, totally ignoring their two-legged friend's attempts to make them return to their hidey-holes. The little boy had no way of knowing his fears for them were unfounded, that the only creature to be in danger was the man; the rats had lots of plans for the older bigger two-legs.

The man was now just outside. Terry stood frozen, listening to the sound of him unlocking the door. It was an old rusty lock, so it seemed to take an age for the key to turn, making a grinding noise like the gears of a car crunching before the unlock mechanism finally did its work.

The man entered the room and looked directly at the boy, oblivious to the dozens of rats moving about the floor. His oblivion only lasted a moment. He was about to close the door behind him when Whiskers leapt at him from the bed just two feet away. The rat easily reached him, using its claws to grip the back of the man's left thigh before stabbing its razor-sharp front incisors through the thin cotton material of his trousers, firmly embedding them in the soft sweaty flesh underneath. The man let out a piercing scream, a combination of intense pain and unexpected shock, no doubt exasperated by the sight and realisation of the black moving carpet of rats about and under his feet.

The man barely had time to catch his breath from the first scream when another rat also leapt at him, this time from the floor but reaching high enough to bite into one of the man's calves. Again, the man screamed, and with pain searing through both legs now, fell to his knees. Dozens more swarmed around him. Some were scratching and clawing at his clothing. Others leapt at him from all directions and angles - upwards from the floor, down at him from the bed and table, some even headlong off the top of the wardrobe. Each found their target with chilling accuracy on some part of the man's increasingly exposed flesh now that so many claws and teeth had ripped away the last of the two-legs' clothing.

Terry still stood frozen in the corner of the room, overwhelmed by what was happening but calmly unafraid, relieved that he was being spared further pain from the man.

Several of the rats were using their strength and weight of their bodies to push the room door further open. Others were nudging at Terry's feet as if urging him towards it. Terry was still terrified of trying to flee, but despite his fear, it was clear the man was in no position to block his escape. More nudging and even nibbling at his toes by the rats convinced Terry it was time to run - and run he did. The frightened little lad ran as fast as his legs would allow, down the stairs, and out the side entrance from the derelict building; through side alleys and streets, on and on not knowing or caring where. Terry just wanted to be anywhere far away from the man as he could get. Eventually, he ran headlong into a policeman who stopped him.

Naturally, the boy was taken into the care of the authorities to ascertain who he was. Doctors, the police, and Terry's parents had tried to coax answers from him. It was no good; he was too traumatised to talk, his young mind finally shutting down for the time it would need to either heal or put up the barriers for as long as it took to come to terms with his ordeal and the horrific abuse he'd suffered.

It was several weeks before Terry was able or willing to speak. He didn't know where, or who had held him. Likewise, the authorities had no idea if he'd been held locally or dropped off in the area.

With no information to go on, for now, the police had no reason to search any of the abandoned derelict buildings in the area. It seemed it was now *the man's* turn to spend some time in the room he'd held young Terry, subjecting the little boy to such pain and degradation. But he would learn - the rats couldn't undo the damage the tall two-legs had done to the smaller two-legs, but they would make it seem tame in comparison to what they would do to *him.*

*

Three days later…

Whiskers decided to move onto the man's testicles. They looked soft and succulent, something the rat confirmed as it bit into one of them, enjoying the texture of the soft flesh and the sweet trickle of blood that accompanied it.

The man screamed the sort of scream no other human should ever have to hear. Even Whiskers was momentarily distracted by it, looking up into the man's eyes. The two-legs was deathly afraid now, maybe even more so than the little two-legged one he'd kept imprisoned in that same room for all those months. It was only a momentary distraction though, and Whiskers returned to nibbling at the testicle. Again the man screamed. This time the little rat paid no attention, more intrigued by the way the little soft balls of flesh were hanging loosely away from the rest of the two-legs' body. He thought about gnawing through the flesh that attached them and taking one to the new-born beneath the floorboards. They would provide good nourishment for Whiskers' young rittens, still suckling at their mother's teats in the space in the walls. Soon though their tiny teeth and claws would emerge and they would be able to feed themselves off the man too, so best perhaps to leave their food in one piece and one place - Whiskers was a good father and would be sure to leave the other testicle for them.

There was still a lot of meat left on the man, enough to feed Whiskers and his companions for a long time, enough even for the next litter of new-born rittens till they were old enough to hunt and scavenge for themselves. But they wouldn't be greedy or rush their meal.

The little two-legs had been kind to them despite the young one's own hunger and treatment at the hands of the larger two-legs. No, they would keep the man alive for a long time, long enough to feel a lot of pain, long enough to pay for all the suffering he had inflicted. It was good the little two-legs had run, to other more caring two-legs who would take care of him - it would have been too much for his young mind to cope with the screams of the older larger two-legs.

They were careful not to gnaw into any of the major arteries, not that thousands of tiny front incisors couldn't easily have coped with tearing a body apart long after *rigour mortis* had set in. But live meat and warm fresh flowing blood were so much sweeter, the flesh so much softer,

The man was now drifting in and out of consciousness. Every so often he would be awakened by more tiny bites and scratches eliciting a response from those nerve endings that were still active. Many of them had already died from over stimulation. The man's vocal cords too had long given up the battle of producing any kind of sound. The man had no choice but to endure his pain in near silence. He was in too much pain to even notice the constant chattering and gnawing sounds of hundreds of rats grinding their teeth. Had he been aware of the noise the rats were making he might have compared it to the excruciating sound of nails being scratched on a blackboard, though one can be sure that would have been a welcome exchange for the reality of what was happening to him.

Whiskers was pleased that the two-legs had lasted so long. He had screamed almost continuously at the limits of his vocal capacity for nearly seven hours when they first gnawed away at his toe and fingernails, exposing the ultra-sensitive areas beneath. All the two-legs' blood had long since disappeared along with most of the flesh.

The thriving colony of rats continued to devour the congealed stuff long after rigour mortis had set in. That still left a delicious taste and smell, an after-taste residue that clung to the bones. It was something to be savoured, like the aroma of a fine wine.

Little Whiskers made the two legs suffer terror beyond human or demonic comprehension before his death. It was of no concern to Whiskers or any of the rats - the man hadn't worried or stopped when Terry Stuart had screamed.

*

The first police officer on the scene was twenty-four-year-old Lee Palmer, a young man who had been a policeman from eighteen and a half years old. In those six years, he'd witnessed his fair share of shootings and stabbings. Even worse, and sadder he thought, was when he had been the first on the scene of the weeks and often months long-dead bodies of the elderly. Mostly it would be the putrid smell of their rotting remains first noticed by the neighbours that would help alert the authorities. Lee Palmer was no rookie.

Nothing had prepared him though for the sight that confronted him when he first entered that room. He felt his stomach start to heave, the bile rising through his throat. There was nothing he could do to stop himself adding to the already unimaginably foul smell when depositing the entire contents of his stomach onto the floor - a man of lesser self-control would probably have added the contents of his bowels and bladder too.

Lying strewn across the bed were the flesh-stripped bones of what was once a human being. Many new-born litters of rittens had feasted on its flesh and bones since the two-legs' death.

***

People Watching

The little mousy brown coloured rat liked living in the city. There were plenty of rich pickings to be had from the discarded rubbish of the two-legs for a smart rat like itself. It enjoyed too the fun of just watching all the two-legs despite for the most part finding their great hulking masses to be utterly repugnant. Too many times, the little rat had come close to death at their hands for it to hold much affection for them.

Nonetheless, they were fascinating creatures, the little rat thought. They came in all shapes and sizes – tall ones, shorter ones (even though they were all giants in the little rat's eyes), fat, thin, and they all looked so different too in their clothing.

The little rat didn't wear clothes of course, but it understood the two-legs' need to – they hardly had any fur apart from a few bits on the head and sometimes a thick covering of whiskers about their faces. The females, it noticed, usually had longer fur and no whiskers, but that was all.

The areas of skin it could see on most of them was a strange pink colour, almost the same as its own kind's new-born rittens.

The little rat would have liked to study them

closer, but most of the two-legs didn't like rats. It remembered one time when it got too close to one, the two-legs had hurled a bottle at it. Mostly though they just made strange shrieking sounds when they caught sight of a rat and would often kick out at it till it scurried away.

On this particular day, it was enjoying a little snooze in a deserted basement, out of the cold. The little rat was unusual, choosing to live separate from most of its kind. It wasn't that it didn't like other rats, it just didn't like the squalid sewers and other places where most of its kind chose to live. That was partly why it understood those 'other' rats' decision to give up the chance of freedom to remain in their warm and comfortable home with the two-legs.

It thought back to that time. A couple of two-legs had found it injured by the roadside some way out of town. It was the rat's own fault, it knew, venturing so far beyond its own territory. In a moment of carelessness, it had almost run into a passing two-legs coming from around a street corner. It had kicked out at the little rat, and on this occasion, it caught the full force of the kick, sending it hurtling into the gutter.

The little rat knew it was probably going to die. The last thing it expected was to be saved by another two-legs. They had even given it a name, Mousey, because of its small size and its mousey brown coloured fur. Yes, Mousey would have been quite happy to live out the rest of its life with them. A part of it still envied the pet rats' luxurious lives, but Mousey was a city rat and a people watcher. The freedom to roam and explore, to hunt and scavenge, such things were in its blood.

*

It had been a bitterly cold and severe winter. The white frozen water covered much of the ground, covering and washing away much of the two-legs' discarded food and waste.

Many of its own kind had died, along with most of its smaller mammalian mice cousins, leaving little for it in the way of hunting. Mousey wondered how it would feed its latest litter of rittens. It was lucky then that the two-legs, Mr Brown, who owned the house and basement Mousey had made a home of, had returned. Apart from being warm, and safe from other two-legs, the one that it belonged to had never laid traps or tried to shoo it away when it caught sight of a rat. And the food it would sometimes leave them, it was tasty and fresh, free of the little pellets that made rats fall sick and die. Even when it saw Mousey's new mate and a litter of newly born rittens, the two-legs had just smiled and let them be.

Mr Brown wasn't like Geoff and Emily, the other two-legs that had helped Mousey. You see, Mr

Brown was a serial killer, a two-legs that really didn't like the rudeness and cruelty of most of his own kind. It was why he sometimes chose to kill those few he took a special dislike to. Mr Brown did however like animals, rats included, which suited Mousey just fine. Mousey, of course, knew nothing of what a serial killer was. What it did know though, or rather what its instincts told it, was that this was a very dangerous two-legged creature. Mr Brown was unlike any other it had yet encountered, way more dangerous even than any of the two-legs that had terrorised Geoff and Emily Jackson. Even the two-legs that had escaped Mousey and the other rodent attackers was no more dangerous than an infant field mouse compared to Mr Brown.

The little rat sometimes wondered, worried even of what might have become of the injured two-legs? Mousey and the other rats had torn out one of its eyes and ripped off half its face before the two-legs had made its escape by jumping headlong through an upstairs window. Most likely was that it had died from its injuries, or maybe of the cold and lack of food – perhaps a combination of all three? Mousey hoped so. It didn't worry for itself, it was quite safe here in the city, but it feared the two-legs might one day return to the Jacksons and the pet rats Mousey had befriended.

*

Mr Brown had been out walking. Mr Brown enjoyed his late-evening explorations of the city. He'd driven to one of the poorer districts, one where the facade of middle-class respectability was nowhere to be seen. There was something almost occult about the contrast of the city lights against the backdrop of the night. As the fading late-evening light slowly gave way to the descent of blackness, it seemed to bring out the seedy and darker side of the city the same way a shower of rain would entice the worms, beetles, and other assorted creatures of the soil to emerge from their domains just below the surface. And so too was it with the human life-forms of the city; the onset of night would see the city's more ignoble elements crawling out of the concrete woodwork to go about their unsavoury activities. To the less observant, the night was no different to the day, only darker. But for the Mr Browns of the world, it revealed so much more: the drug dealers earning money for their business-like suit-clad suppliers, the pimps and ladies of the night touting their wares, the pathetic junkies out to score their nightly fix, though not before they had perhaps robbed some poor unsuspecting innocent to pay for it. Such human flotsam both fascinated and repulsed the unassuming serial killer in equal measure. But so long as such creatures didn't bother him, Mr Brown adopted a live and let live attitude. He expected the same in return though, and when that uneasy truce was broken, Mr Brown didn't hesitate in making such violators pay for their mistake. This was such a night …

Mr Brown had spotted a somewhat dishevelled looking man slumped in a doorway, partially illuminated by a street light. At first glance, he looked much like any one of society's many other forgotten and abandoned casualties. Mr Brown would probably have stopped and given him some money for a meal had he asked politely. Instead, the man *demanded* such a contribution from Mr Brown. There was an air of menace about him. Mr Brown stared at his face. A makeshift blood-soaked bandage adorned the upper part of his head, wrapped down and round to cover the left eye and part of his face. A closer look showed it to be little more than a dirty piece of rag really, and not the sort of dressing he would have gotten in a hospital. The man repeated his demand …

"Well? You gonna cough up then? Would be better for you if you did." The threat was accompanied by the production of a hunting knife.

"The answer is no," was all Mr Brown said in reply, utterly unconcerned by the implied threat of violence. The slightest trace of a smile started to form around Mr Brown's lips in anticipation of what was now sure to follow. It was all coming back to him. Mr Brown remembered reading about three escaped prisoners holding an elderly couple hostage a few months back. There was some fantastic garbled story about two of them being attacked and killed by rats. The third was still at large but was believed to have suffered an injury to one of his eyes. The one who had escaped was a particularly nasty piece of work by all accounts. He had robbed and killed a young shop assistant in a botched robbery, Mr Brown seemed to remember reading. The world would be a better place without such a loathsome creature.

Without so much as removing his hand from his jacket pocket, Mr Brown thrust the six-inch carfentanil-coated dart into the man's midsection. The initial shock of the sharp stabbing pain was all the distraction Mr Brown needed. He used his other hand to follow up with the application of a hefty dose of chloroform to the man's mouth, immediately rendering him unconscious. But it was the powerful immobilising elephant tranquilliser on the dart, albeit heavily diluted, was what would keep the man unconscious once it started to take effect a few minutes later.

*

The little rat once again peeked out from behind a drainpipe, looking up at all the people. A passing two-legs spotted the little rat and picked up a rock-like stone to throw at it. The throw missed by a fair distance. Mousey rasped a mocking hiss at its would-be assailant before retreating back behind the drainpipe, reminded yet again what evil creatures most of the two-legs were. It was then that the little rat's attention returned to the house from which it had ventured.

Mr Brown was returning home. Mousey followed him to the garage where the two-legs was parking the metal box it sometimes rode in. Given the tasty treats the two-legs sometimes provided its rodent tenants, Mousey was pleased to see the return of the strange two-legged one. The little rat was even more pleased when it saw it dragging the body of another of its kind from the back of the metal box. But the smell of death about the other two-legs was not yet total; perhaps it would be feeding them *freshly* killed meat this time? There was something that intrigued Mousey too, something familiar about the smell of the other two-legs. The little rat was confident it had encountered it before, it just wasn't sure where?

Mousey and his hungry brood of rittens watched it chain the other two-legs to the metal piping that kept the rats warm in the basement that it allowed them to share. Their anticipation of a delicious meal was heightened by the smell of fresh blood that filled the air. Mr Brown had used the hunting knife the man had used to threaten him earlier in the evening to slice away his tongue - it just wouldn't do for the man's screams to disturb the neighbours. Nor would it have been fair to distress the little creatures whose home the man would be sharing for the rest of his short life with when he returned to consciousness.

Mr Brown left the now chained and naked man in the cellar to become more acquainted with his fellow inhabitants there. Mousey was the first to creep towards the unconscious two-legs. The little rat finally recognised the smell, and now the one-eyed face of the two-legs before it. At least Mousey knew what had become of the last of the two-legs that had terrorised the elderly two-legs who had been so kind to it all those months ago. The little rat was pleased it no longer had to worry about it returning to seek vengeance on them and their cute little pets. Not only that, but Mousey, the latest litter of little rittens, and all their cellar rat friends would be eating well that night and for several more to follow. Perhaps the Jacksons weren't the only good ones after all? Mr Brown wasn't too bad either …

***

Lab Rats

Little Terry Stewart was now that writer's cliché, a strapping young man, and no longer the frightened little boy who had once been held captive by a sick paedophile.

It was a policeman walking his local beat who Terry first ran into after his escape from the man and the room he had been kept a prisoner. But Terry always remembered Whiskers and the other rats as his real rescuers from that evil bastard.

It was only thanks to advances in DNA identification fifteen years later that the police had been able to identify the remains of who Terry had only ever known and thought of as 'the man.'

Michael J. Holby was his name, not that it mattered now. Terry Stewart had put the past behind him, resolving to move on and make a success of his life. But he never forgot the debt he owed his little friends, determined to repay their kindness one day.

*

Terry was considering a job offer from Rateznox Genetics, a biogenetics company, for a laboratory research post. He had mixed feelings about the role. He knew it would involve his handling of rats for scientific experimentation, even dissection possibly.

Terry did lots of research into the company before deciding. Some of the projects they were working on had potential far beyond a few medical breakthroughs for humans. It was always the case that any new drugs would be tested on simple mammals first, so why not ensure a few of his 'friends' enjoyed the benefits too? He would never allow the rats he worked with to suffer or come to any harm as far as he could. And just as determinedly, if the opportunity arose to do anything to help them, advance them to the point they could better survive a human-dominated world, then he would - and what better place than a laboratory researching cellular enhancement - rats had cells too!

He accepted the job.

It was a real Deja Vu moment when Terry first saw the new batch of rats for their current research project. One of them, the smallest and youngest by the looks of it, was a tan coloured infant male. Despite it being smaller and younger, he recognised it immediately as being the image of Whiskers, the little tan rat that had befriended him so many years before. He christened it *New* Whiskers.

The old Whiskers was the one that with the help of his other furry friends, had undoubtedly saved

Terry's life when the rat hoard launched their attack on the man, his captor.

'The man' though, Michael J. Holby, hadn't fared quite so well. Not surprisingly, despite Terry still having trouble sleeping because of those two years captivity, the man's gruesome fate wasn't one of the things that kept him awake at night.

Terry knew instantly that this was one rat no one was going to prod or poke or do anything to that might hurt it. He thought about releasing it into the wild but knew that a rat explicitly bred for lab research would not have the skills or instincts to survive among naturally born wild or city rats. He decided he would instead smuggle it out and look after it himself.

Working at the lab was harder for Terry than he expected. He hated the experiments and dissections the lab rats endured and thought many times about jacking it in. He didn't though. It would have been different if he could have taken all the rats with him or get all such places closed down, but neither was going to happen.

Nonetheless, he remained determined to repay somehow the debt he owed Whiskers and the others all those years ago. Terry buckled down to his work.

One year later …

Terry was aware New Whiskers was a significant way through his life. Already the ageing rat was showing signs of the many illnesses rats were prone to – breathlessness, wheezing, and the beginnings of a tumour. Thanks to his practically encyclopaedic knowledge of rat physiology, Terry had so far been able to treat the rat successfully. But he could not halt the inevitable. Sooner or later his little friend was going to die.

It made sense then, Terry having a keener than usual interest in a new and exciting line of research his lab was working on, that of cellular life-extension. Other labs were working on it too, but Rateznox was way ahead of the curve.

"Ahrr!" Shrieked Nick Hughes, one of the junior lab technicians, "the little shit just bit me."

Terry suppressed a smile. He didn't like Nick. Neither did the rats. He thought the man was a twat, the rough and careless way he handled and referred to them.

"Don't worry. The little fella's not infectious or dangerous in any way. Hand him over, and I'll put him back in his cage while you go and sort yourself a plaster," Terry told him.

"Sure, "Nick answered, "just a sec though." He raised the rat up to eye level and made an angry snarling sound at it. It was clear the little rat was terrified, and in pain too judging from the squealing it was doing.

"For fuck sake, ease off. It's just a tiny defenceless little animal. It can't hurt you!" Terry shouted before taking the rat from Nick's hands.

"They bug the hell out of me. I've never liked rats, horrible little fuckers they are."

"Then why the fuck take a lab assistant job in a research laboratory like this, then?"

"For the money, and it'll look good on my CV for when I eventually move on." Terry intended that time would come sooner rather than later.

Nick's cruelty towards the rats continued over the coming weeks. It wasn't vicious or life-threatening, nothing Terry had grounds to complain to the lab supervisors about, but nonetheless, he hated the way Nick treated the lab rats, teasing them at every opportunity. It was time to put a stop to it …

"You fancy coming over to mine this evening? I've a bird coming over, but she's got her sister in tow and asked if I had a mate I could invite over to make up a foursome. You interested, Nick?"

"Sure I am," Nick answered, "provided she's a looker."

Nick called at Terry's flat bang on seven that evening. Terry explained that the two non-existent women were running late and wouldn't arrive for another half hour or so. Terry handed him a beer he'd already opened to ease his disappointment.

Working in a research laboratory provided Terry with all manner of anaesthetic and sedative drugs, a hefty dose of which he'd discreetly deposited in Nick's beer.

Living on the ground floor of an old Victorian house meant he had access to a deep and spacious basement with exclusive use of the garden, both of which had been useful in his caring for the large population of rats that he cared for. It helped too that the rest of the house remained empty what with it being pretty much unliveable from decades of neglect; it was why the lease for the ground floor flat had been so cheap – the situation suited Terry just fine.

Within twenty minutes, Nick was barely conscious. Terry was surprised at just how quickly the drug concoction he'd slipped him took effect. He was grateful too of being spared the tedious task of having to make further excuses about the non-arrival of the female bait he'd used to lure Nick in the first place.

Terry set about dragging his unconscious co-worker's body to somewhere he'd be 'less' comfortable when he awoke, namely the deep space he'd excavated in the soft-brick basement floor. Nick's body landed with a bit of thud when Terry rolled it into the man-sized pit, but the generous layering of hay and straw ensured he wasn't injured.

Halfway up the sides, Terry had sculptured a sort of ledge all the way round to place a makeshift roof to Nick's final resting place, much like the lid of a coffin.

What made this pit unusual were the rat-sized tunnels leading into it from either end. They would at least allow a healthy air supply, ensuring the occupant didn't suffocate – Nick didn't know it yet, but that would have been a preferable end to the one Terry had in mind for him.

It was a slow and horrible death. On the plus side, Terry's feed bill for all his rats for the next month was next to nothing …

*

The drug trials of the cellular life-extension serum had proved more successful than any of the Lab team Terry was working with could have hoped. Little was said about Nick's unexplained disappearance from their number, and it had left Terry free to conduct his own research free of Nick's watchful eye.

The research Terry was working on was of course highly classified, but his position allowed him unrestricted access to all the experimental drugs Rateznox Genetics hoped to profit from in the future. He made sure New Whiskers was the first unofficial recipient of the new serum, praying that it would save and extend the little rat's life. Within days of administering it, the ailing rat's health was not only restored but had seemingly rejuvenated it to a younger and fitter self. Once he was sure of no ill-effects, he gave the wee rat a dose of another compound Rateznox was working on, a serum for increasing synaptic responses in the brain. Again, the results were as swift and equally remarkable. New Whiskers' increased intelligence was off the scale; the usual 'seeing how fast a rat could navigate a maze' tests were practically an insult to New Whiskers' abilities. Terry soon found that New Whiskers could respond to verbal commands such as *sit, go here, go there*, and that was just the beginning. It was difficult to accurately measure the rat's new intelligence since no such tests existed for it. By trial and error, Terry established the rat had acquired a rudimentary understanding of spoken language – not just tone, body language, or other such cues, but actual words and sentences.

For the most part, Terry had kept New Whiskers

separate from the other rats in the basement and garden, but he needed to know if these new traits would be unique to the rat or if they would be passed on to any offspring. Needless to say, the rat jumped in every sense of the word at the opportunity to be placed with a couple of young does.

Less than two weeks later, New Whiskers was a proud 'daddy' rat. This surprised Terry. The gestation period for a pregnant rat was usually between 21 and 23 days, over a third longer than for New Whiskers' rittens. And just like their dad, they immediately started exhibiting signs of superior strength and intelligence.

After the rittens' birth, along with New Whiskers, Terry kept them separate from the other basement rats – he wasn't ready to unleash hordes of *Rattus Superior* on the world just yet.

*

Terry's new 'super rats' weren't the only supposed super rats in existence. Increasing use of various poisons, each more lethal than the last, was leaving subsequent generations of the creatures more and more resistant to the deadly weapons man was using to kill them. Reports of rats the size of foxes were a common occurrence in the media. Terry knew the stories to be hysteria-inducing exaggerations, but in the mind of an already rat repulsed public, they helped fuel the hatred of them.

In response to the problem, Rateznox Genetics had been awarded the contract to come up with a new and more potent poison to significantly reduce their numbers. It came up with the idea of a viral-delivered nerve agent targeted explicitly at the rats' respiratory systems, something they were prone to suffering with already.

This new development forced Terry to face a dilemma that had been troubling him for some time; much of the work Rateznox was doing provided exciting potential for enhancing the rats' survival abilities. On the other hand, they were also likely to make their human tormentors smarter, and longer-lived too

Terry knew that despite all the genetic enhancements he'd given his family of rats, they would still be no match for an equally endowed human population. Most of his own kind had an inherent revulsion of rats. He feared Rateznox's development of a more virulent and effective rat killing virus, that his fellow humans would exterminate them from existence.

Terry was determined to at least give them a fighting chance. He knew what he had to do.

*

New Whiskers scurried out of the burning building, unafraid of the flames dancing about him. Not even the thick smoke was bothering him, with nothing but the purest oxygen filtering through to his enhanced lungs and bloodstream.

With his new lease of life and all the genetic enhancements his two-legged friend had given him, the first thing the GM rat was going to do was breed.

At the rate rats reproduce, New Whiskers knew his GM genes would be dominant throughout the country within just a few years. And with the rats' historic ability to colonise any ship afloat, the coming rodent apocalypse would be worldwide.

Fifty years later …

Terry was sitting in his garden, listening to the singing of the birds, and watching the rich array of wild-life all about him. He'd moved into a quaint country cottage in the Peak District just a few years before to enjoy the area's natural beauty; he could easily have stayed put in London though - the entire world was mostly one big National Park now.

A rat was nibbling away at a piece of cheese Terry had placed there on the garden table for him.

Terry noticed a little greying around the ears and temple, and a certain slowness of movement. It was to be expected. New Whiskers was now extremely old for a rat. Terry watched several dozen more happily playing and scurrying about in all directions, unafraid of the enormous two-legs in their midst. There was no reason for them to be afraid. Rats were now the dominant species on the planet. Most had never seen another human apart from Terry, and nor were they ever likely to.

Terry was one of the last few humans left alive …

*** *

Ship Rats ...

It was the year 1845 when on the morning of the 19th May, the British Royal Navy captain, Sir John Franklin, set sail with 133 of the finest British sailors aboard and in command of two of the equally finest ships, HMS *Erebus,* and HMS *Terror.* Both were equipped with the latest sea-faring technology of the day, to map the Northwest Passage.

It was only because of the dishonourable discharge of five seamen from the crew before their final departure from Disko Bay off the west coast of Greenland that any of that expedition was to survive at all.

"You're a lucky man, John, I would give my right arm to be joining you," Sir John Franklin's long-time friend and fellow Arctic explorer, Sir George Back, was telling him on the day of the expedition's departure from Greenhithe, England.

"I wish you were. For what it's worth, I think the Admiralty were absolute fools not to have selected you for in the first place for this, George."

"I heartily agree with, John," George replied, "and for that reason alone I think they have been right in their decision to choose you instead."

The two friends both laughed in unison knowing that to be the truth.

No expense had been spared in preparing for the expedition. Compared to the previous sail ships of the first expeditions two hundred years before, they were a sight to behold. With their powerful locomotive steam engines, iron-plate bow reinforcements, and a host of crew comforts undreamed of by the press-ganged sailors of those same earlier expeditions, these were super ships.

Added to those impressive preparations was grain, tinned and dried foods, and enough other provisions to feed the eventual 128 men of the two crews for the next three years. They would also nourish many more times the number of rodent stowaways that invariably found their way aboard every large vessel that had ever set sail.

*

The two ships had been at sea for over a year, and it had been hoped the weather would be milder now for the time of year. It wasn't.

A couple of the older ship-hands were the first to fall ill with the fever. It didn't seem that serious at first. A certain amount of sickness was to be expected during any long voyage, even several deaths given the cold and icy conditions they were sailing in. It was assumed a few days in their bunks and the doctor administering to them, they'd soon recover. They didn't. The fever steadily got worse before the doctor noticed the reddish-purple blotches around their throats and faces. Closer examinations revealed foul-smelling fluid-filled pustules across their chests and abdomens. The doctor ordered the two men quarantined at once, not an easy task aboard the close confines of a ship. Within a week, three more of the crew and one of the officers were also sick. And even more frighteningly, whatever it was, was also aboard their ominously named sister ship, *The Terror,* also reporting two crewmen with similar symptoms.

In the bowels of the ships, many new litters of rat rittens had been born. With such vast provisions held in the food stores, life was perfect for the ship rats, barely having to scavenge at all. Such was the sheer vastness of the non-human areas, the rats were able to share their accommodations without the two-legs being aware of either sight or sound of them. But the rats sensed that not all was well with their two-legged shipmates.

All the two-legs now carried the sickness in them. Many of them had already died. To minimise contact with the dead, their bodies had been swiftly thrown overboard rather than being wrapped and weighted for the more traditional burial at sea; no doubt the departed would find a more permanent resting place, washed up along the icy shoreline.

Others were still a long way off the stage they would start to suffer but it was just a matter of time, they carried the sickness. Only two had lived through and recovered from the fever, and even on those two, the rats could still smell the disease infecting them, one they would inevitably pass onto others of their kind.

The rats had seen sickness like this before. Since many thousands of litters ago, their inherited memory of the Black Death persisted, when the rotting bodies of the two-legs stretched as far as the sun lit up the ground.

Several of the men were more resistant to the virus than the others and of course, those who had already died. It was entirely possible that several might live long enough to reach the port of New York. If that happened, they would certainly pass it on to others who would again pass it on and so on across the world. But even if they didn't, the two that had recovered would definitely infect others, it would just mean the sickness would spread a little slower.

Another two more of the crew died of the mysterious disease, and the ship's doctor was still none the wiser as to the cause or a cure. With no other explanations being offered, someone suggested that it might something spread by rats. With such unusually large areas of the ship to hide, the rats had mostly managed to stay out of sight. The crew and officers knew from experience though that 'out of sight' didn't mean they weren't there.

Every sailor alive was aware that any vessel bigger than a small domestic boat would have its fair quota of rats managing to find their way aboard. And so it began, the laying of traps and poisoned grain where they knew the rats would find it, and the soaking of the wooden beams with the foulest rat repellents.

The last prong of the crew's efforts was flooding every recess and corner of both ships with thick charcoal smoke to flush them out even further. Hundreds of rats succumbed to the crew's hunting and killing of them.

The sudden rage of the two-legs towards the rats was a mystery to them. Then again, most things to do with the two-legs was a mystery; they set traps for them, hunted them with dogs and ferrets, left foul food out that put them to sleep, and the white-coated ones, they did all manner of strange and painful things to them. And yet still they were the rats' most valuable friends and allies. The two-legs provided them with all sorts of delicious foods and treats to scavenge among their garbage. The two-legs had even dug vast networks of tunnels for the rats to roam and take shelter from the cold beneath the cities where most of the two-legs lived. And in the country too, the farms and villages were like giant food stores to the rats, free and permanently open to them.

There were millions of more two-legs in the world now than in those past times so another sickness like the Black Death would kill equally many more. The rats knew if the two-legs died in such numbers, so too would their own kind; all the waste and garbage the two-legs produced and threw away was the rats' greatest food source.

They couldn't afford for the two-legs to die in such vast numbers without sacrificing as many of their own.

Even with their best and cruellest methods, the two-legs' efforts at trying to rid themselves of the ship rats, for each one they trapped or poisoned, a dozen more were born.

With a much-reduced crew, Captain Franklin knew their only hope was to return to civilisation and receive the proper medical help and care they needed. Accordingly, the captain ordered the remaining crew of HMS Erebus to abandon ship and join him aboard HMS Terror before setting sail for New York, the nearest city and port with the facilities that might save them.

Such was the fear of the disease now, the bodies of the dead and even some of those in the later stages of dying were left aboard as they were.

With the fate of one of the ships now decided, the rats had only HMS Terror and its crew to deal with. The sturdy construction and iron-plating of the bows made it impossible for the rats to sink the remaining vessel merely by gnawing away at the weaker and more accessible parts of the respective hulls. It was imperative though for their own kind's broader survival that HMS Terror should not only never reach New York, but that it should also never escape its present icy wilderness. Such a sturdy ship, even with its crew all dead could easily drift for years until salvaged by some other passing vessel. The rats knew that a disease didn't always die with its host.

With nearly two thousand rats aboard, they out-numbered the remaining two-legs by some 40 to 1, and many of those were closed to the point of succumbing to the lethal disease. It was the time of year when the skies darkened early. Their black and brown fur would be difficult to detect in the blackness of the night when they launched their attack. They knew the captain to be the dominant male among the two-legs. He would be their first target …

Though the iron-plate bow of the ship made it

impossible for them to sink it, most of the internal walls and beams were still wooden. It was easy for the rats to gnaw and scratch their way into the captain's cabin. The captain was taking a much-needed rest in his bunk. Silently and with great stealth, the rats climbed up on to the structure on which he lay. Perhaps a hundred of them were now crawling on and all around the captain's body. He stirred, aware of what at first seemed like an itch moving about his skin. And then he felt the pain. A rat had taken the first bite. Its teeth had sunk deep into his neck. Whether by accident or design, the bite had severed a vital artery. Blood gushed from the wound. Many of the rats were startled at their sudden drenching in the disease-ridden liquid and scurried away. In fact, they all made their escape, knowing their job here was done.

All over the ship, the rats made similar attacks upon the weakened and diminished crew.

One of the advantages the two-legs had over them, apart from their greater size was their better eye-sight, even in the dark. The rats knew this, and so mostly it was the eyes they went for first. The immediate horror and pain of tiny incisors piercing and rending eyeball flesh from their socket sent victims into a literally blind panic. More than a dozen had now fallen that way to the rats' tactics. Terrified screams filled the bowels of the ship.

At least half the crew had not been asleep when the rats simultaneously launched their vicious assaults and were clutching whatever makeshift weapons that came to hand. In a terrified frenzy, they thrashed and struck at their rodent attackers, killing dozens in the process. But there were just so many. The rats swarmed the remaining crew from every direction, leaping to bite at their calves. Others literally dropped from the ship rafters onto their backs and shoulders. The worst of the attacks were from those that landed on face and neck - biting, scratching, and clawing at the most exposed and vulnerable areas of their victims.

The feeding orgy that followed lasted for several days. Actually eating the diseased flesh of their meal would most likely pass on the disease and kill the rats too. The rats knew this, but it would be a quicker and better end than slowly starving and freezing to death, or eeking out a few more weeks of life by reverting to cannibalism.

The rats had intended that their own dead bodies and the remains of the crew to stay hidden in the cold and ice-covered world that surrounded them. And they might too were it not for the effects of climate change leading to their discovery almost two centuries later.

*

It had been a mystery comparable to that of the Mary Celeste.

One hundred and twenty-eight experienced seamen had just disappeared along with the two state of the art expedition sailing vessels on which they had set sail.

It seemed though that the 170-year mystery of what had become of the Franklin expedition was apparently solved. In 2014, the Victoria Strait Expedition found HMS Erebus, and then two years later the Arctic Research foundation Expedition discovered its sister ship, HMS Terror. Both had been enclosed in ice off the northeast coast of Canada.

Until then, the fate of that ill-fated expedition's ships and their two crews had been speculated on at length, not only in the scientific and sea-faring communities but also in the world of literature, most notably in the writings of Jules Verne and Mark Twain.

Both the investigative and literary ponderings were as fascinating as the wildest imaginings the mind could conjure - but the truth, that was something quite again. It was strange as it was frightening, and a story yet to find its ending …

*

Five years later …

... News reports are coming in of several deaths in Northern Canada from an as yet unidentified virus ... Scientists believe a dormant virus may have been reactivated by the warmer temperatures following the thawing of ice sheets along the Northern Canadian coastline. A number of dead bodies have also been discovered in the now melting ice. Professor Markham of the Canadian Institute for Arctic studies has speculated that the discovery of the Franklin Expedition ships back in 2014 and 2016 may have reactivated the suspected virus during their investigation and retrieving the previously ice-enclosed vessels from their frozen prison. Aboard those vessels, the remains of many more, though mutilated bodies were also found ... scientists have yet to make any progress with either classifying or creating any kind of vaccine for the currently unidentified virus and are warning of a potential pandemic unless drastic quarantine measures are imposed across North America ...

Ten years later ...

The humans had hoped to stem the pandemic by isolating themselves in their homes, hospital wards, and finally gigantic quarantine zones. It was all too late of course.

The rats though, albeit in reduced numbers, they're doing just fine. Despite the loss of most of their human benefactors, they continue to thrive among the ruins of a once dominant species.

**

Screams in the Cellar

The main entrance had been boarded up years before, but being an old building, there was a myriad of other little nooks and crannies through which the rats could come and go. Through a combination of man-made and rat dug tunnels and pipe-work, they were able to bring the obscene creature its food. But it was getting bigger and more demanding. The small dead animals they could take it were no longer enough to satisfy its growing hunger. They would need a means of bringing it larger prey …

*

There had been rumours about the old house for several years, ever since that young fella, Terry Stewart, who used to live in the ground floor and basement flat before he disappeared.

They had in fact started sometime before then. The neighbours had thought him a bit creepy. There was nothing anyone could say for sure, just a feeling. He had been some sort of scientist at that laboratory place. He'd disappeared round about the same time it had mysteriously burnt down.

The fact that Terry had lived there in the first place made him stand out all the more. It was an old, dilapidated place, run down and practically derelict looking, the sort of place you might expect squatters or homeless people to be taking shelter. Terry though had been clean and tidy, easily earning enough to live somewhere nicer.

Several of the rats Terry Stewart had saved from the Rateznox Genetics experiments were still living there, one in particular, a sickly one he had taken pity on. When it hadn't responded as they wanted to the growth serum the Rateznox scientists had been administering it, Terry's boss had ordered its destruction. Terry noted at the time just how insistent they were about that. There seemed a sense of urgency in the order too that the rat should not only be terminated, but its body utterly destroyed. They wanted no trace of its remains to survive.

Terry hated the casual way they referred to such things – they wanted it killed – *murdered* in his eyes. He had felt sorry for it. There was no way Terry was going to give it that last lethal injection or be a party to its little body being unceremoniously tossed into an incinerator. He chose to take it home instead. It joined the others in the basement. It hardly moved, just sitting there, its melancholy mood and pensive look on its face rarely altering. One thing that was changing though, Terry had noticed, was its size; both Terry and the basement dwelling rats would bring it food. This was unusual behaviour for rats, Terry knew.

Usually, rats would abandon and even turn on one of their number showing signs of being sick or diseased. Not with this one; they had deferred to it in a way ants or bees might to an egg-laying queen of their species. It hadn't been long before Terry didn't have to do anything for the fast-growing rat, seeing the others were attending to all its needs – feeding, cleaning, making sure it was comfortable.

Terry had no idea just what had been in the serums the rat had been given while at the laboratory, probably steroid based growth hormones he'd assumed, at least at first. Whatever it was, it had him worried. He'd dreaded to think what Rateznox would be doing with the monstrously sized rat if they could have seen it just a few short months later.

Terry loved his little friends. He always had since those terrible days of his youth when they had rescued him from the horrors of his time being held captive by 'the man.' But he found it impossible to feel anything for this one. It was grotesque looking. It smelled foul. There was a constant drool of viscous mucus about its mouth and whiskers. And though Terry was not swayed by appearances alone, there was something malevolent about it … something evil. He had feared just what sort of monster it would eventually grow into if it continued its current rate of growth and mutation?

Terry never learnt the answer to that question. It was soon after that he disappeared following the 'accident' at Rateznox Genetics. But the rat remained in the abandoned house, continuing to feed, growing ever more grotesque.

Terry had been right, to a point, about the growth hormones Rateznox had been giving it. There had been something else in them too – genetic material from another similarly growing rat on the other side of the world, a descendant of the mythical giant rat of Sumatra alluded to in several literary works, including those of Conan Doyle.

The Indonesian island of Sumatra itself also happened to be where the Rateznox Genetics corporation had its Head Quarters. It was also where they carried out some of their most dangerous and controversial research, free from the inconvenience of international scrutiny or indeed that of their own government. The giant rat of Sumatra was no myth the corporation had discovered, but a real living breathing creature. It was also a mutation, brought about by god knows what - radiation, previous undocumented experiments, or just some freak of nature? No one could be sure, but what they did know was that it was a festering cauldron of disease.

It was only its remote location hidden away in the depths of the Sumatran jungles that had prevented the diseases it was incubating exploding on the island's population, and then probably beyond. Rateznox Genetics knew the risks they were running in bringing blood and tissue samples of it to their UK facility, but that's where the expertise and facilities were to further their research. They hadn't allowed for the apparent accident that befell their UK lab. They didn't know that thanks to Terry, another strain of the mutant giant rat of Sumatra was living and growing in London.

*

The rats knew they had to move the giant one of their kind when they heard and smelled the two-legs scrambling about those rooms above the basement, knowing they would soon descend to their basement domain.

Typically it would have resisted the others' manhandling of it, but it too could hear the noise from above, instinctively knowing it meant danger to itself. To the other rats' surprise, for they had never actually seen it move before other than to twitch and scratch at its whiskers, the giant one started to shuffle. They nestled beside it, adding their strength and weight in helping it down into the drainage tunnel in the corner of the basement. Like most of those rats Terry had brought home, many of them were far from ordinary. With their unusual intelligence, they had anticipated the day when they might have to escape or hide the giant one in a hurry. Several of the strongest had already used their strength and numbers to raise and push the man-hole cover to the side. As soon as the monstrous rat was out of sight, some of the others pushed it back. They hoped that would discourage the two-legs from investigating further in that direction. Their own discovery and perhaps sacrifice was of little importance to them.

The rats needn't have worried. To the untrained eye, the rats appeared just like any others. It was nothing more than a cursory search of the house for clues to Terry Stewart's disappearance following the suspected arson attack where he worked. Apart from being revolted at seeing several of the repulsive vermin scurrying about, the police investigators were indifferent to them. The feeling was mutual …

Without Terry providing food, the rats feeding the growing mutant one were having to source it themselves. Rats were generally good at that with their hunting and scavenging skills. But the supply of small mice and other food they were able to scavenge from the two-legs was struggling to keep up with the giant one's growing size and appetite. Already they had had to move the giant one back into the central area of the basement to accommodate its increased growth. And the giant one's tastes were changing.

To feed its hunger, the rats were now bringing it larger prey – with so many of them and being exceptionally strong, the basement mischief found it easy to overpower cats and even small dogs and foxes, dragging them back to the giant rat's basement home. Quite often the food they brought would still be alive, just the way it preferred. It was unfortunate the house was not always empty of human occupants; there was something tragic and horrible about the sound of a defenceless animal being mutilated by powerful teeth and claws while the grotesque mutant mass feasted on its flesh. It would have been a mercy had the giant rat gone straight for the head or heart, but it never did. It would invariably start on the legs or stomach, somehow knowing that would ensure the poor creature would live just a little longer through the ordeal.

The poor creatures' screams would echo through the house, more often than not causing the occasional tramp or homeless person taking shelter in the derelict rooms to flee.

It was those homeless people that gave the giant rat a new taste. The rats could hear and smell the latest new ones living above. The weather was terrible, and there was little in the way of live flesh on the streets for the rats to hunt. That didn't diminish the growing one's hunger or need to feed though. The giant rat was no longer satisfied with discarded scraps from the two-legs' rubbish to supplement its feeding, it had to be fresh, preferably still alive.

The two-legs above would make for easy prey. The sort who usually took shelter in the rooms above were invariably weak, sometimes old too. The mutant rat directed its minions to bring them.

It would be impossible to drag their greater size through the established network of tunnels and pipework they used for smaller animals. They started gnawing at the thick wooden basement door and 'keep out' boarding that the police had re-erected after their futile search for Terry Stewart.

The rats possessed a strength that belied their size, as did their long sharp teeth. It didn't take them long to gnaw a human-sized hole through the door and barricades. They already knew there were at least three of the two-legs on the other side, two males and a female of their kind, not that they cared about that last bit. A couple more were lying asleep on one of the upper floors

The two-legs the rats knew of were in what used to be Terry's living room. The two-legs were burning some wood for a little warmth. Fire was one of the few things that truly frightened the rats, but it was enclosed in the fire-grate, so they paid it little attention.

They slowly crept about the room, increasing their numbers behind the sofa, the sideboards, and atop the bookcases. They were cautious at first; for most two-legs living in a regular house or flat, the sight of a rat in their lovely home would have them reaching for the nearest weapon to attack it. Not these ones. Any that the two-legs did spot crawling about they tended to ignore. They were used to squalor and having to share the streets on which they usually slept with such creatures. All they cared about was enjoying the comfort of a roof over their heads, somewhere to sit and escape the world in a drug and cheap alcohol filled daze. One could only hope they were in such a state now – it might dull the pain.

The rats slowly emerged from their many hiding places about the room, unconcerned at being seen now. They surrounded and outnumbered their prey many times over. Their apparent numbers and presence were enough to alarm the homeless trio.

"What the …?" one of them startled to mumble, "they're coming from everywhere," he added with more urgency.

"Arhh," the female one shrieked when she felt one of the rats brushing past her leg before biting into it. She tried to rise and kick it away with her foot. That one little sign of resistance triggered their onslaught.

From all around the room, the rats descended on them. From the sides, leaping down from the bookcases, even up from beneath the floorboards. The three victims were literally being drowned in a sea of fur, teeth, and claws. The three two-legs fought harder than the rats had expected. Fear and panic had awakened the trio from their cheap cider induced stupor. Despite their weakened condition, when faced with certain death they had found a new and unexpected strength when trying to fend off their attackers, something the rats would remember and make allowances for in future attacks.

It was no use of course. The rats had prepared well for their first encounter with a more formidable and stronger prey, quickly overwhelming them by sheer weight of numbers. In their ill and malnourished state, the two-legs' initial newly discovered vigour was soon exhausted. In less than five minutes, though still struggling and continuing to put up a token resistance, the fight was lost. Punctuated by shouts and cries of pain from the incessant biting, the rats were already dragging them in the direction of the hole they had gnawed in the basement barricades, ripping away the filthy lice-infested ragged clothing along the way.

The giant one looked favourably on the new food source his minions had brought it, its whiskers twitching and vibrating in anticipation. A slime-ridden puddle of the newly exuded viscous mucus it slobbered over live food had formed all around its grotesque mass. It had a strangely paralysing effect on any living creatures it came into contact with, robbing them of their strength and ability to move.

The now naked two-legged victims were being dragged and rolled in it in preparation for what was to come. The last of their resistance passed, the giant one plunged its face into the mid-section of the first of them, using its proportionally larger talon-like claws to rip away at the two-legs' flesh. It liked to rend its food into smaller portions for easier digestion. It would have been a kindness had the paralysing agent in the mucus robbed the victim of all feeling, like pain and the ability to scream. It did not.

Two of the victims had to lie motionless, listening helplessly to the pitiful cries and screams of their friend. They had never imagined such a monster could exist. They wished now they hadn't ignored the rumours about the screams from the cellar of the house they had taken shelter in. Any concern they had had for their friend evaporated as the last of her was swallowed in the giant rat's jaws, knowing they would be next. Just a few remnants of her remained, the smaller rats having their fill of what was left.

The remaining two legs cried and pleaded for the

rats not to attack them, to have mercy, let them go, anything but the horror they had just witnessed. Their pleas were falling on deaf ears; unbeknown to them, the rats fully understood the two-legs' words. The older ones though also remembered their time in the Rateznox laboratory, of the injections, even the dissections of their siblings. The two-legs would find no mercy among the rats.

When the last of the two-legs had been disposed of, the giant one and its subordinate mischief basked in that satisfying feeling of having fed so well. For the first time, even the giant one forgot its constant hunger for more.

It had another effect too; the giant one was no longer the almost immobile mass that had been entirely dependent on its subordinates. The human nutrition had brought about yet another mutation. Its proportions had become virtually normalised, making it look more like a regular rat, but a thousand times bigger. This normalisation though didn't diminish the terror any sight of it would inspire. However less hideous it might have appeared since this last seemingly more benign mutation, it had the look of a far more vicious and dangerous creature too. This new incarnation could attack and fight in its right rather than relying on its army of smaller minions. It wanted more of the two-legs' flesh, more than might be supplied by the few who occasionally dared venture into the creepy house above. It was time to move on …

It was the brief pause in its craving that allowed the other two-legs in the house to escape. They had heard the piercing screams of their fellow itinerants in the depths of the house. At first, the anaesthetising effects of their own drinking session had dulled their awareness of what was happening. That dullness was probably amplified by their *not* wanting to know, the comfort of being under a proper roof being stronger than their growing fear of the rumours they had also heard. But the sight of a few curious rats scurrying about in their own part of the house was enough to bring them to their senses and hastily leave the supposed house of horrors.

It was the first time the homeless people's reports of what they heard was finally taken seriously. The police search of the premises was more thorough this time. The dried slimy mucus, the blood, the bones still with a few traces of flesh on them, it all made for a scene far worse than any of the experienced, hardened officers had seen or ever imagined.

*

It was a complete mystery. Not just who but *how* the tunnel had been dug, right from the sewers directly into the basement?

The question they should have been asking was *what* dug the tunnel *from* the basement to the sewers …

The screams had stopped. Whatever it was had gone … *but where?*

*

The giant one was many miles away with the mischief horde of smaller rats at its command. From the safety of the sewers and long-forgotten tunnels beneath the city, they could now strike and feed on the two-legs at will. The monstrous size and strength of the giant one had enabled it to dig many more to accommodate its ever-increasing size.

It and its minions would make valuable allies for the other mutated lab and other rats of all kinds in the coming war …

***

Circus Rat

Mr Ratty was the star attraction of *Ludvig's Little Big Circus*. It was one of the few circuses that had not only survived but increased its popularity in the face of the public's changing attitudes towards live animal performances. Despite the circus animal trainers' care and devotion for their performers, the public had been convinced it was all exploitation. Pictures and film footage of the theatrical use of whip cracking with the more ferocious stars, lions and tigers mostly, portrayed the traditional circus as cruel and barbaric.

Strangely though, this cry of exploitation never extended to the smallest of the circus's animal kingdom stars. The flea circus remained a firm favourite, along with the glass-sided ant colonies and other assorted creature attractions. But for Ludvig, the undoubted star and money spinner was *The Amazing Mr Ratty*, as the advertising posters portrayed him.

Ludvig's Little Big Circus had been touring three years back, not long after when the Rateznox Genetics facility went up in smoke in mysterious circumstances. By sheer coincidence, the circus had been performing in a local park a few miles from the site at the time.

Ludvig had been enjoying a rare day away from circus business, strolling through one of London's many open and semi-wild park spaces. He'd spotted a squirrel that had managed to get one of its legs tangled in some twine or string. Ludvig couldn't be sure exactly just what it was he was seeing, but it caught his attention. A rat had approached the squirrel and immediately started gnawing away at the string or whatever it was. Despite its predicament at being unable to escape what was holding its leg, the squirrel had turned to try and scare the rat off. The rat in its turn had looked up, then spat and hissed loudly, utterly unafraid, its body language clearly aggressive. The squirrel resumed a passive stance, visibly afraid. The rat continued its gnawing of the string. Moments later, it was shredded through, and the squirrel was free. Before scampering off, the squirrel stood still, like it was hesitating, not sure of what to do.

For what seemed an age, though in reality just a few seconds, the two creatures eyed one another up. The squirrel then shot off faster than Ludvig's eyes could follow. But it wasn't the squirrel he was interested in. The rat's actions had fascinated him. He knew from his experience with the circus that a lot of animals had a sense of altruism towards one another. Even among unrelated species, some were known to care for another's young or come to their aid. He'd never seen such evidence in a rat though, not that he'd had much experience of them. There was something different about this one, something rare and unusual. He wondered …

Again, Ludvig's experience with other animals stood him well. He made no sudden movements or did anything that might scare the rat away. The rat he was watching stared back at him. It was no more afraid of the two-legs than it was of the squirrel it had just helped. The rat was appraising the two-legs, just as it knew it was doing the same. Ludvig threw a small piece of chocolate in the direction of the rat. It landed a few feet from where he had dropped to one knee to coax the rat closer. The rat responded just as he had hoped. The rat knew what the two-legs was trying to do. It was unconcerned. Unbeknown to Ludvig, the rat had seen him before at one of the circus performances. It had also observed him with some of the few remaining small animals there. It knew the two-legs wasn't one of those that hated rats, so again, it approached closer, allowing the two-legs to take hold of him.

And the rest was history as they say. Mr Ratty, as Ludvig called him, proved to be every bit as intelligent as that first day when he saw it in the park.

It would be wrong to say Ludvig trained Mr Ratty to perform the remarkable tricks it did; all the circus owner had to do was demonstrate the slightest indication of what he wanted, and Mr Ratty immediately understood. It wasn't long before Ludvig realised he didn't even have to do that, that the rat understood being *told* what to do. Not even the most complicated of tricks, like performing the spinning somersaults off a diving board was beyond Mr Ratty's immediate understanding. He suspected, no, *knew* Mr Ratty's intelligence and abilities went far beyond mere circus tricks.

Mr Ratty sometimes thought it amusing how smart the two-legs all thought he was. There were moments though when he found it patronising - pushing cotton reels round a track, jumping off miniature diving boards, running back and forth on a silly see-saw, and also the fantastic shows of strength when Mr Ratty would either push or drag a cannonball. It was all so mundane, hardly worthy of his superior strength and intelligence. And yet … Mr Ratty revelled in the attention he got. A part of him loved performing. He was the star of the show.

Over the next few years, Mr Ratty's extraordinary intelligence and trick performing made him quite the celebrity. That had not been his intention.

The many normal rats that followed the circus for whatever nutritious left-overs it provided sensed there was something different and extraordinary about Mr Ratty and would show due deference. But Mr Ratty knew he wasn't the only such 'extraordinary' rat in the world, that he was not unique. Often, he would see others of his 'special' kind watching his performances from a discreet distance, clearly not impressed. A few were indifferent, but most resented that one of their own special kind should be playing the part of a performing seal for the two-legs' amusement. It was also clear they were keeping a watch on him, regardless of how far and wide the circus travelled. Though he was yet to fully understand his still-developing abilities, he could sense and even feel their disapproval from afar. It came as no surprise when one lone rat approached his cage following one of the nightly shows Ludvig's circus was doing … this one did not show deference.

"… Those same humans that applaud and laugh at your demeaning tricks are the same ones that are just as happy to see others of all our kind tormented and experimented on in all manner of hideous ways. And for what? To create a new shade of cosmetic for their females to paint their faces, or maybe to test the toxicity of ingredients in a new shampoo. It matters nothing to them if every other life-form has to suffer or even die for their vanity?"

There was no sound, but Mr Ratty heard in his mind what this other rat of his special kind was saying. It was using the two-legs' own words and language too. Mr Ratty wanted to reply but wasn't sure how? Oh, it knew *what* it wanted to say, just not *how* to make itself understood in the other rats' mind in the same way.

The other rat could see Mr Ratty's thoughts and answered them.

"If you hadn't spent these last years learning and performing the humans' tricks you would have learnt all the new things we have."

Mr Ratty paused further to think on the other rat's words. It remembered the time when it accidentally nipped at the skin of one of the white-coated lab assistants at Rateznox. The two-legs had squeezed its body and screamed in its face. Mr Ratty remembered he was still barely a ritten at the time, and how terrified he was.

The other rat was still monitoring Mr Ratty's thoughts and reactions.

"Yes, that's right. That human would not have hesitated to crush the life from your tiny body for that one solitary moment of discomfort you caused it. Think then what experiments they would perform on one of us with our new abilities? To the humans you perform your simple tricks for, you're just a novelty – but to the white-coated ones at places like Rateznox,

and the rulers of the humans, you're a threat. Our coming war with them will be hard fought - we need time to amass our numbers, to develop further, and to prepare for that time. Your daily and nightly demonstrations of our abilities would deny us that time if you were to come to their attention. This must stop!"

Mr Ratty had realised by now the other rat was reading his thoughts. He didn't yet know how to transmit his own the way the other rat could. For now, it didn't matter, knowing too that all he had to do was think of what he wanted to say and the other rat would pick up on it.

"... We know that not all humans are bad, ones like your Ludvig or the one among the white-coated scientists at Rateznox who helped make us what we are, but as an entire species, they are nature's biggest mistake. We intend to rectify that mistake."

Just then, both rats heard and smelled Ludvig coming towards them ...

"There you are wee fella," were Ludvig's first words when he caught sight of Mr Ratty scurrying around the open-air enclosure he had set up for him, "time to get you back in your cage."

Mr Ratty would have liked to remain and listen to more of what the other one like him had to say. For the first time, Mr Ratty felt lonely. He was different from all the other circus animals – not just because he was a rat and they weren't. *The Amazing Mr Ratty* knew and could do things they would never be able to, it was why Ludvig kept him. He knew quite suddenly how much he needed and wanted to be with his own kind, not just other rats but ones like himself, 'special' ones.

Mr Ratty turned to look up at his human keeper. He had never thought of Ludvig in those terms before, but now he did. Ludvig provided his food and water but also kept him in a cage at times or at least within the general confines of the circus.

Now Mr Ratty may not have been able to directly convey his thoughts to that other rat, but he had developed a similar sort of ability with Ludvig. Their communication had long since transcended mere sounds and gestures. Ludvig often knew, perhaps instinctively, Mr Ratty's mood or something he wanted like food or water, when he was willing or not to be picked up or handled in any way. It wasn't as precise as what was exchanged between the two 'special' rats, but there was certainly a sort of exchange of thoughts going on. This was the moment of truth to see just how far that went …

Ludvig stopped in his tracks. There was something different about Mr Ratty. The remarkable little rat was troubled, unhappy about something. Mr Ratty stared up at Ludvig, then turned his head to gaze at the world beyond the restrictive garden-like enclave Ludvig had created for him. He knew in that instant Mr Ratty's time with the circus was coming to an end.

Ludvig didn't know how, but he knew many other things too. A whole swath of thoughts now filled his head. The unspoken communication between them had never been so clear and precise. There was regret on both sides. Mr Ratty had enjoyed his time with Ludvig's circus, but there was a war coming, and he knew which side he had to choose. Ludvig also knew of the coming war now, not that anyone would believe him, at least not *yet*.

They agreed that the remarkable little rat would stay with the circus one more night, just for old time's sake.

It was to be Mr Ratty's best ever performance … and his last. Ludvig was going to miss him.

*

Ludvig now lives in a remote corner of the Scottish Highlands. The day after Mr Ratty's final performance, Ludvig had signed ownership of the circus to its performers.

He wanted to be as far away from the coming troubles as he could …

***

Plague ...

Remember that plague back in 1347, you know, the one that decimated a third of Europe, the Black Death? - 75 million people according to history? Yes? That's the one ... that was us ... well, a rather *special* one of us, the most demonic rat that ever lived, but that's a longer story for another time.

We rats had enjoyed over 700 hundred years of prosperity during the dark and middle ages following the fall of the Roman empire. But you were finally emerging from them, a stronger and even more industrious species. It was time to cull your numbers once more, just as it was over 300 years later when we again struck at you with another black death, the one of 1665 that your Daniel Defoe wrote of with such eloquence.

And then there were the ten plagues of Egypt - Yes, that's right, even way back then, that was us too, nothing to do with Moses; our primordial brothers and sisters among the Nile rats were immune to the Egyptian plagues we were to infect you with, having evolved together and alongside the biblical pestilence.

We're the single most successful killers in your history. The words 'rats' and 'plague' go hand in hand, like sword and shield, good and evil, and yes, even life and death.

We're not saying we didn't have a bit of help along the way over the centuries to follow ... two world wars, the Spanish Flu, famines ... but us rats are the best pestilence carriers ever to walk the earth. The worst biological nightmares your scientists can brew up in your laboratories and little test-tubes are nothing to the misery we can spread.

Oh yes, we know all about those. We spend enough time running your mazes from A to B, having to suffer electric shocks for bits off cheese, being prodded, poked, and dissected - we know all too well about the two-legs' laboratories. And just for the record - we don't like them!

You seem puzzled by all this, wondering why we kill so many of you? Why we would want to decimate a species that produces enough waste for us to scavenge and feed our young, that builds vast tunnels and underground passages for us to hide and take shelter from the rain and cold?

The answer is simple. With your greater intelligence and technology, you're like children playing with fire, genuinely believing your place at the top of the food chain is yours by right. Without us to check your numbers from time to time, you would destroy us all. The truth is, it is *you* who are the plague upon the planet.

*

Had the Roman Empire been allowed to dominate and unite the world, there would have been no limit to how far or quickly you might have progressed, what you might have achieved. But the advancements you briefly enjoyed thanks to the Romans were more than you were ready for, just as your current technology is beyond your wisdom. We could not allow it, not then, and even less so now…

The Roman Emperor Marcus Aurelius Antonius ruled over two-thirds of the civilised world in the year 165 AD. There wasn't a power on earth that could stand against Roman might … and yet … for the next fifteen years, he had to watch as we decimated Rome's numbers, made him watch as some 2000 of its finest citizens fell to us each day in the worst of those times. By the year 180, we had lessened their numbers by over 5 million.

Unlike its citizens and even its mighty emperors, it was us who ruled and enjoyed the freedom of the empire.

The humans' numbers had steadily increased to levels rivalling our own. This had never bothered us in the past. The more the humans multiplied and spread across the land with their houses and villages, the more waste and places they produced for us to scavenge and take refuge. But the Romans' incredible ingenuity was slowly killing us - better sanitation, barricades preventing our entry to many of their homes, and proper disposal of their garbage to places we couldn't reach. They were all combining to threaten us with starvation while driving us from our homes. We faced being forced back into the wilds to compete with our natural enemies for food and shelter, enemies with teeth and claws as sharp as our own. We had to act.

Living alongside the humans and what they left behind, taking refuge in the strange structures they built, it had all made life good for us, a life we had gotten far too accustomed to give up now … We had learned from experience that provided their numbers didn't grow too many compared to our own or if enough were sick or wounded from all their wars, they posed little threat. Humans were at their most wasteful and useful to us when fighting or dealing with other such disasters. We could create such disasters …

It started in the Mesopotamian city of Seleucia, an area the humans now call Iraq. Some strange new disease had taken hold, the Antonine Plague or Plague of Galen as it would also be called in later years. It had left many dead for our new-born rittens to feed on.

With the breakdown of their ordered lives, there was much to scavenge, and no place left that was easy to bar us from. But the surviving Roman soldiers would soon go, and those left behind would quickly die. There would be much feasting for a time and then more scavenging as we sifted through the last remains of the human things - but then there would be nothing, and we too would die if we stayed. Instead, we climbed aboard their grain and supply carts when they left, hiding in ways and places unseen by human eyes. With our help, the soldiers would carry the disease back to Rome, creating more carnage for us to scavenge in the aftermath.

The disease killing the inhabitants of Mesopotamian had been nothing for us to fear, it was strictly a human killer. In the city, it had mainly been the tiny flying things that the humans call mosquitoes, hovering over the sewage-filled rivers and lakes, that had brought death to them. But they were not the only carriers. We too could bring death this way as could the fleas that nestled themselves in our fur. A few of us bit and infected several of the soldiers while the little flying things we harboured infected the rest, particularly those already suffering from minor infections and fever.

Within a few short years, we had spread the

plague back to Rome, to Gaul, and the legions along the Rhine. By the time we were done, we had decimated much of their entire empire.

On his deathbed, Marcus Aurelius sent for Galen, the imperial family's Greek physician … "This disease will continue to spread long after my death and into the reign of my son, Commodus. I look to you, Galen, to find a cure, to stop it before it destroys everything we've built and our dreams for the future."

Galen had shared Marcus Aurelius' fears. Not only was the disease killing Rome's people, but it was also threatening to plunge Roman civilisation back a thousand years. All the advancements, culture, and the very march of progress were at risk.

Galen was ahead of his time in suspecting the disease was being carried and transmitted in numerous ways. He believed the main culprit to be rats though, a creature that knew no borders, and whose dominance of everywhere they went was more complete than any Roman legion's could ever be. But Roman emperors were rarely receptive to being told their all-conquering armies were powerless against such a thing. The present emperor, Commodus, was no different. If he'd had his way, hordes of gladiators would have been sent to do battle with the disease bringing vermin, as if man-made iron swords and leather shields were enough to slash or defend against death itself. Wisely, he took Galen's advice and used one of nature's own most potent weapons – fire. Villages, towns, and when that wasn't enough, even entire cities were put to the torch in trying to stem the Antione plague.

The disease did indeed eventually subside, but a hefty price had been paid in the halting of it. Tens if not hundreds of thousands died in the great burnings, both humans and rats. Some of Rome's and the world's greatest minds had been among its casualties. Many great libraries and other repositories of learning and culture had been lost to the cleansing but all-consuming pestilence dousing flames.

With their numbers thinned, Rome had become reliant on auxiliary foreign armies to fight their wars. It was the beginning of the end of Roman power, heralding the Dark Ages, a time of widespread warfare and intellectual darkness and barbarity. And amid the centuries-long chaos that followed, we rats were to thrive and rule supreme.

*

You've come a long way since those dark days, but your wisdom has not. It will take another such decimation to allow time for the latter to catch up … Ebola, SARS, Rodent Flu … it's just a matter of time, and *we* shall be the carriers.

Karni Mata's Teeth ...

The three land rovers' legendary off-road capabilities had certainly been put to the test in their journey across India to Rajasthan. The three occupants, one in each of the now tired looking vehicles saw their destination coming into view, the small, dusty town of Deshnoke, midway between New Delhi and India's western border. From a distance, it was a decidedly unremarkable looking place compared to the rest of the marvel filled sub-continent. It was only as they got closer their senses really became attuned to the feeling of strangeness in the air. It wasn't anything they could put their finger on, but it was real nonetheless.

The specific place in Deshnoke that interested them was Karni Mata – Temple of the Rats. Tourists and devotees of the goddess Karni Mata travelled from all over the world to visit and pay tribute to the 20,000 or so rats living in the temple, or *Kabbas* as they were called, meaning 'little children' in the local dialect.

The three men, on the other hand, their interest was neither tourism or paying their respects. They drove to a nearby hotel to park and rest up for the night.

*

Sharumi, the elderly caretaker of the temple and their guide for the day, addressed those visiting the temple for the first time …

"The temple's story stretches back more than 500 years. It began when Yamraj, the god of death, came for the soul of a 10-year-old child, one that was much loved by the goddess, Karni Mata. Refusing to allow the taking of the child's soul, she turned it into a rat, one that would eventually follow the usual path of reincarnation."

Among the usual flock of tourists and devotees of Karni Mata listening that day were the trio of land rover driving adventurers. They were not so usual, and far from benign in their interest in the temple rats. They had gone to great lengths to blend in among the crowds, but the rats sensed otherwise. The inlaid marble floor was alive with the revered kabbas. They appeared indifferent to the giant creatures towering over them, all except for three men whose feet they purposely skirted round. It was like the out of place trio were surrounded by some repellent, deterring the rats from scurrying about their feet the way they did with the rest of the visitors. The rats' seeming avoidance of them went unnoticed by the other visitors. Many of the group the men had attached themselves to were also first-time visitors to the temple and somewhat skittish as they attempted to navigate their way through the seeming undulating blanket of fur moving about the floor. There were others too who were not so skittish; barefooted pilgrims would sit among the rats, silently playing with them, sharing and eating the same food, allowing them to sit on their laps. The pilgrims and devotees were never fearful of being bitten. Sharumi had told them that never in the temple's history had such a thing occurred.

Had any of the temple staff noticed the absence of rats about the men's feet they might have put it down to the trio merely taking extra care for fear of injuring or even killing one of the kabbas underfoot. It was after all one of the first things visitors were warned of, that these were no ordinary rats, but the earthly representations of the goddess Karni Mata herself. To kill one was considered a mortal sin, and any who did, even accidentally, was obliged to atone by replacing it with a statue of gold or silver.

Over its 500-year history, the temple had amassed a veritable fortune in such atonements and other offerings, not including the fabulously valuable solid silver gates. It was these priceless gates through which visitors had to pass to make offerings to the hundreds of rats that at any one time would be scurrying about the base of the sacred silver statue of Karni Mata in the shrine at the heart of the temple. It was this magnificent prize and the many others that interested the three men the most, not being sure yet how they might acquire the gates as well given their size and weight. Still, that was what the three separate land rovers were for should there be a way, and if not, they still expected the statues on their own to make the job worth it. The one of Karni Mata alone would make them rich.

They continued making a pretence of listening to what Sharumi was telling the party of tourists they had joined …

"One of the theories about the temple rats is that they are the reincarnations of the children of Karni Mata. She was a 15th-century sage and healer who disappeared from Deshnoke at the age of 151. Karni Mata was revered and loved for her goodwill and boundless generosity. She was also endowed with supernatural powers. And while there are a variety of tales as to how the mass of rodents came to live here, all tell of the goddess reincarnating a human child's soul as a rat."

It was the mention of supernatural powers that caught two of the men's attention …

"Special and indeed magical among these rats are the white ones of which there are only three or four out of the twenty or so thousand living within these walls and thought to be reincarnations of the goddess herself and her four sons. So, you see, it would not just be a simple rat you killed if you should trample one."

Jason, the leader of the three, was uninterested in what Sharumi was saying, dismissing most of it as legend and superstition. The other two were less sure. Like Jason, they were from Europe, but they had spent a lot longer in India, long enough to know there was a lot more to India's mysticism and mythology than mere storytelling for the tourists. They listened to the last of Sharumi's history of the temple ...

"Deshnoke stood alone in Rajasthan in being untouched by the worst ravages of the plague when it came. Those who visit and make pilgrimages to the Karni Mata Temple do so not only to worship the rats but to also heal whatever troubles them."

The city of Deshnoke felt blessed in its possession of such a revered and holy place.

The temple was the rats' home, both physically and spiritually. It was also their sanctuary; in the open space inside the temple, a large overhead net served as a room, protecting the rats from being caught and carried away by the many cheel birds hovering above in search of an easy meal. The temple was a place of sanctity and reverence for the people of Deshnoke, and indeed throughout India. It was perhaps these factors that led to no thought of any practical security ever being given for it and the fabulous treasures it was reputed to house deep in its underground chambers. Such an oversight made it a tempting prize for those outside the culture and legends that had given birth to such a holy place.

*

It was a joy to see the harmony that existed between the temple rats and all those that came to visit and pay tribute. No one suspected another side to the rats' nature, one that belied their small size and apparent friendliness. All except the elderly caretaker, Sharumi, that was. He was one of the few who knew their true power; apart from the story of the rats being the reincarnations of children, there was another one attributed to them, a less romaticised one that the temple staff didn't tell the tourists.

Sharumi smiled while he went about his duties, putting out food and milk for them. It was only a little while earlier that devotees were drinking from the bowls the rats bathed and played in, eating too the crumbs of food the rats would leave behind. And later, many would return to sleep in the temple, allowing the rats to crawl about their bodies throughout the night.

A small white one was watching Sharumi, also smiling in its own way, sensing the time of the old man's passing was but a few years off. The white rat knew the temple's caretaker would soon be joining the vast family he had devoted his entire life to caring for – it wasn't just the souls of children that were privileged, or in rare cases, cursed in such reincarnations to the temple.

*

"It's not going to be as easy as we thought. Who needs security when those bloody rat worshippers are there night and day practically?"

"True. We may have to leave the silver gates behind, but we always knew that. But there is a way. We can lace the rat's evening milk with a sedative, which should also knock out the weirdos who share their food and drink before sleeping in the open courtyard with them," Jason told his two associates.

"And what of Sharumi?" asked the third one of the trio, "he's up and about from four in the morning till eight at night. He might be old, but he'd fight to the death protecting those rats and the temple statues?"

"Then die is what he'll do. I'm not letting some rat-loving old man interfere with us and getting our hands on the statues or whatever else of value they keep." His two cohorts looked to one another with concern. They hadn't figured on killing anyone. On the other hand, they knew Jason, was right, there was too much at stake for half-measures if they ran into problems.

The three men made their preparations. They'd quickly realised that trying to sedate the rats' milk wasn't practical as not all those who slept in the temple would drink enough to be affected. They, or rather Jason, thus decided on a more extreme measure.

The entire temple was riddled with an intricate network of pipe-like tunnels, rat-ways for the rats to explore and move about their sanctuary. It was the perfect delivery system for flooding the place with an anaethetising agent. It probably wouldn't knock out all the rats, there were just too many of them, but it would be enough to render the human occupants unconscious if they directed it towards the courtyard where they slept. They would deal with Sharumi separately if necessary.

*

They scheduled their raid for the early hours of Monday morning, the region's holy day of the week. It was even more fortunate that it coincided with one of the region's many religious festivals and the temple would be closed for the holy day. They figured too it would increase the time before the theft of the temple treasures was discovered.

The three land rovers were parked to the rear of the temple, away from the busy streets to the front. The lack of conventional security made it easy for them to enter through one of the small wooden entrances there, with plenty of foliage and natural cover to obscure their activities. Once in, the trio crept along its hallways towards the central courtyard and pathway to the inner shrine where the silver statue of Karni Mata was kept. They knew from previous visits it lay just ahead. The three of them split up to different rooms adjacent to the courtyard. From their earlier watch on the temple, they estimated only about five or six people were sleeping there, less than they had expected, though still too many of them to take on. They donned their gas masks before rolling the quick release gas canisters inside several of the rat-way tunnels, some of which were sure to lead to where the devotees were sleeping. They also hurled several more in many other tunnel entrances, hoping to knock out most of the temple rats. They didn't want them swarming about their feet or drawing attention by fleeing from the temple when they started to remove the valuable statues.

More than half the rats had succumbed to the sleep-inducing gas. The ones that hadn't though were enraged at the desecration that was taking place, and the assault on the child reincarnated kabbas that had already taken place. They were less concerned with the attempted attack on themselves, it was their destiny to face such dangers.

Despite their rage, there was a forgotten joy in

their warrior spirit being awakened after such long dormancy. They scrambled over the sleeping bodies of their fellow creatures. In addition to being sworn to protect the rat reincarnated children, they were also the guardians of the fabulous wealth of the temple, the sacred offerings and gold and silver statues that had been accumulated over the centuries in the atonement of those rats that had died before their time.

The temple thieves carefully navigated their way through the mass of sleeping rats, and the few devotees now sprawled about the courtyard. The solid silver gates to the inner shrine were too big and cumbersome to even move let alone remove so they passed them by towards the silver Karni Mata statue. Behind the silver figure was another door, a solid silver one much like the gates only smaller. It was heavy, but between them they managed to pull it open, discovering the heavily worn stone steps leading down to the basement chambers where more treasure was supposed to be stored. Jason led the way down …

"It's an Aladdin's cave down here," were the first and immediate words out of Jason's mouth. His two fellow thieves nodded their agreement, too mesmerised by the wealth of treasure to speak. What they saw was beyond anything they could have imagined. Hundreds more gold and silver statues adorned the shelves that had been carved out of the chamber's marble walls, many of them embedded with priceless jewels. Most were miniature representations of various Hindu gods, small enough to be carried. Some though were of rats as big as themselves, way too big to take with them.

There was no way they would have time to remove them all, not even the smaller ones, but enough to make them rich beyond their dreams. As soon as they got over the initial shock of the chamber treasures, they each started to grab at those statues they could carry away with them, unaware of the silver door slowly closing behind them at the top of the stairs.

Despite his age and being alone, Sharumi was slowly pushing it closed though not quick enough before the three men became aware of the light from above closing on them.

"Quick you two, the old caretaker must have woken," Jason roared, scrambling up the stone stairway, "he's trying to shut the door on us."

It was too late. The network of rat-ways the rats used to move about the temple extended down into the treasure chamber also, even alongside the stone steps. It took only a few of them biting at his feet to send Jason hurtling back down them. Hundreds more were emerging from the many other tunnel entrances and from as many different directions, swarming the chamber-robbing humans. With the door above now fully closed, their flashlights weren't enough to fully illuminate the chamber in which they were now trapped. The darkness made the rats' poor eyesight more than a match for the humans, and with their vast numbers, they were all over them. They used their teeth and claws with the same deadly intent as they once did their kirpans, the traditional swords and daggers of the Sikh warrior soldiers they once were.

The trio's death was mercifully quick though a far from painless one. The rats were already eating their fill before death took them, human flesh making a pleasant change from the milk and vegetarian dishes the temple staff and visitors provided. There was soon little of them left but bare bones scattered about the human blood-stained floor.

The rats were sworn to protect the chamber, and that included not leaving it desecrated with any trace of their enemy. They lapped up the blood like it was nectar and carried off the skeletal remains back through their tunnels. By the morning there was no earthly sign the three men had ever been there unless, like Sharumi, you knew what to look for.

*

The story of the rats being the reincarnations of children was right, but only in part. Thousands more were also the reincarnations of Sikh warriors, the fiercest of India's fighting men and soldiers, there to protest the kabbas and temple treasures from just such threats the would-be temple robbers posed. At least once in every human generation, someone was foolish to try and steal the wealth of Karni Mata.

Sharumi was showing the latest group of visitors around the Karni Mata temple of the rats, giving much the same lecture as always did on such occasions. Among the visitors was a successful career criminal with ambitions of pulling off yet another profitable venture. He was listening to Sharumi's lecture to those visiting for the first time, that part of the address the three thieves of the previous month would have done well to pay more attention ...

"And part of the legend says, those who deliberately harm the rats and steal from the temple, they too shall be reincarnated as rats, solid gold ones, their minds and souls forever trapped in a lifeless prison to atone for all eternity."

The warrior reincarnations among the rats eyed the would-be temple thief with suspicion, waiting to fulfil their protective role ... after all, they had three more human-sized gold rats to protect now.

***

Super Rats

It was one of the oldest parts of the original sewer system, running deep beneath the city of Cranberry. It was no longer used, well, not officially. Modern and more efficient drainage pipes carried the city's human waste to the new recycling plant out beyond the suburbs. Some of it seeped into the surrounding land but not enough to be a problem.

It had not been entirely abandoned though. It was now home to literally tens of thousands of rats. The absence of human droppings from it made for a safer refuge from the dangers of the human two-legs living above the surface. But nor had it been *entirely* abandoned by its human builders either.

Much of Cranberry's wealth had once been centred around manufacturing and food processing plants; there were many other sectors to the economy now, but the former still provided half the city's tax revenues and continued to hold a lot of pull in its running.

One way in which they exercised their influence was in 'encouraging' the environmental officials to turn a blind eye to some of their practices. There were many plants and factories dumping their industrial waste products into it. A high-pressure water-flushing mechanism was still in operation, sending this new waste to join the human sewage from the drainage pipes farther along the system.

Most of it was harmless to the rats, and that which wasn't, they adapted to. The bulk of the industrial waste came from just one contributor, the city abattoir. Many of their discarded meat products were considered too dangerous to remain in the food chain, even as pig feed. You see, this particular abattoir also handled carcasses from various farms and ranches. Most had pumped their animals full of steroids and growth hormones. Others had been fed on experimental GM crops, and God knows what else before their eventual dispatch to the abattoir. By rights, it should all have been classified as Bio-Hazard material and disposed of accordingly. But that would have been expensive.

Oddly enough, most of this discarded meat never reached the main sewage flow where it might have added considerably to the negligible contamination from the regular sewage.

The illegally disposed of meat was another attraction for the rats. Tons and tons of protein-rich food had allowed the sewer-dwelling rats to give up their surface scavenging. Their ever-increasing numbers were growing bigger and stronger with each new litter of rittens, most which had ever seen a human two-legs. The few that had were indifferent to them. These new generations were not afraid of the two-legs …

*

"I tell you, Bert, they're fucking huge, and they don't run from you like regular rats do," Alan Rickman was telling his supervisor.

"Well, I ain't never seen 'em, not the sort you speak of, and believe me, I've seen my fair share over the years. You sure it wasn't sommat else you saw, you know, like a dog or something?"

"Nah, they sounded different, they made that sort of clicking and scratching sound rats do, and they sort of, you know, hissed when they saw me."

"I'll come out with you on the next quarterly inspection. In fact, we'll get a whole team together. We need to either find out exactly what's down there or put an end to all these stories. Each time I hear one, the rats are bigger than before."

Alan nodded his agreement, reluctant to further discuss his latest sighting. Bert too wondered if he'd been a little hasty in his determination to find out the truth. There had been too many similarly told stories for them all to be exaggerations or a trick of the light.

Alan and Bert both worked for the city's waste

management department, and that meant they were the ones responsible for the periodic inspections of the old sewage tunnels. They were supposed to venture right to the heart of the system, but none did.

For several years, rumours of the sewer-dwelling rats had grown quicker than the rats themselves. If the most graphic were to be believed, you'd be picturing rats the size of Doberman dogs. They weren't that big, at least not yet, but many were twice the size of a domestic cat or the urban foxes that crept about the city. The term super rats was increasingly being whispered.

Added to their monstrously increasing size, the rats had developed grotesquely protruding incisors to tear away at the constant supply of drug-riddled meat. And likewise, with their claws, they too had grown proportionally. They were more like talons now, capable of rending a man's eye with a single swipe. Alan and Bert were not looking forward to the forthcoming investigatory patrol.

With so many new litters being born, the rats were running out of space. Even the old and uncharted network of natural caves deep beneath the original sewer tunnels were fast filling with more and more of them. The caves were why the sewers had never over-flowed or become blocked, providing extra drainage for the high-pressure water-flushing used to propel the industrial waste towards the regular sewage. It had always baffled the Sewage Department why the system worked so well. They were unaware of the long-forgotten caves and had never thought it necessary to waste money on investigating – if it was working, no point in trying to fix it.

For the sewer rats, the increasing lack of space was becoming more urgent. If these had been normal rats, they would never have reached such numbers. The over-crowding would have been settled among themselves, killing off the sick and the elderly, even some of their own young. But these weren't normal rats. There were no sickly ones among them, and the eldest were every bit as strong and vicious as their younger offspring.

Food was becoming a problem too. There wasn't a shortage exactly, but the seemingly endless supply was having to stretch farther and farther with each new litter. But these rats were not inclined to kill a single one their new-born rittens.

The time they all knew was coming was almost at hand ... there was plenty of space beyond the limits of the old tunnels towards the surface – where the two-legs lived.

And food too, there was a world of food to be had there. The rats had grown tired of eating the discarded dead carcases. Their appetites were changing.

Though most had never seen a two-legs, they instinctively knew there to be as many or even more of the fresh warm-blooded bodies than themselves.

The few scout rats that had ventured to the territory of the two-legs reported them to be weak and afraid. Yes, they were big in size, but they were mostly weak and had no claws or teeth with which to fight. They would make for easy prey was the rats' thinking.

*

"... news reports are emerging of a significant reduction in the number of homeless to be seen on the streets. However, this is not due to any efforts on behalf of our housing and welfare services. It has long been known many homeless men, and some women too, use the entrances of many dis-used sewage tunnels for shelter and to sleep in, returning to the city during the day to beg or look for food. But over the past week, less and less are returning ..."

The recent reports of the mysterious disappearances of many of the city's homeless, and speculations that they were somehow connected with the sewer tunnels had the locals in a panic. Alan and Bert were among those most alarmed. They would be the ones leading the forthcoming inspection, brought forward by a month because of the current situation.

"Well, this is it, mate, into the lion's den we go," Alan joked. He and Bert, and the other men in the inspection team approached the entrance to the tunnel where most of the city's homeless were known to enter the vast network of sewers for shelter.

"I only wish it were just lions we were dealing with. Lions you can see, lions are big bastards that attack you in the open. Rats though, they're sneaky fuckers, crafty and vicious … who's idea was this again?"

Alan laughed at the reply, adding: "I see you've lost your enthusiasm for this little jolly almost as much as I have."

The local media had wanted to send in a TV crew to accompany the inspection. The city council though, not wanting their lax enforcement of the industrial and other waste disposal regulations exposed thought it prudent to refuse. As an after-thought, they imposed a blanket ban on speculative reporting of the situation, i.e. no more 'Super Rats' headlines.

This tunnel entrance they intended to enter wasn't one that had been inspected in over thirty years, so no-one quite knew what to expect. The only reason for doing now was because of its known popularity among the homeless as shelter.

The inspection team were barely a dozen feet inside the tunnel when they saw the first signs of human habitation. There were a few makeshift tents, and the remains of cooking fires were evident. Also evident were many large rat droppings. More disturbing was the way whoever lived there's bits and pieces had been left randomly like they had been tossed about in a panic. Closer inspection showed blood stains scattered about the ground and walls. The question now was, do they continue as planned and report their findings later or request more specialist backup. Alan and Bert's preference would have been to call in the army to go ahead with ruddy great flame-throwers, burning every rat they found, whatever its size.

"Let's not jump to conclusions, there's been enough of that already. Continue the inspection as planned," Bert's boss on the other end of the phone told him.

The six-man team continued past the makeshift homeless camp. Another ten feet saw the tunnel start to twist to the right and they lost most of the light streaming in from the entrance. That problem was remedied by their head-mounted touches attached to their hard hats. What they couldn't do anything about was the loss of their cell-phone signals. The density of the granite surroundings would make short-wave radio communication equally impossible. They were on their own now.

The ground was mainly composed of soft earth and clay, and an abundance of moisture gave it a sort of muddy feel underfoot. Farther in, the tunnel narrowed considerably, and the six men found themselves having to stoop their heads and shoulders.

After many years of disuse, the stench of sewage was no longer the stomach-churning experience it had been in the past, but still, remnants of it hung in the air. There were other smells now, almost as bad. There was the unmistakable aroma of rotting meat; they had encountered it many times before in previous inspections of other parts of the tunnel system. It was common knowledge the local abattoir still flushed their waste through the redundant sewers, so it was not unexpected. But there was another smell, new to them. It was the smell of death.

The farther in they travelled the stronger it became, replacing entirely any lingering reminders of the sewage. As they ventured not just farther along, but deeper as the downward gradient steadily sharpened, they found the slow trickle of filthy muddy water slowly rising to above ankle height. It seeped in from tiny fissures in the walls, and more from the auxiliary network of rat-sized pipework – normal-sized rats that was, not the monstrously large super rats of the rumours.

All the team were donned in their personal protective equipment or PPE as it was called, so it wasn't an immediate problem. What did alarm them were the torn scraps of flesh floating in it about their feet. They wondered too about the changing colour of the deepening water they were wading through, becoming more and more reddish the farther they walked. Another thing they noticed was the strange 'static' like noise steadily growing in volume with each step they took. No one cared to admit just how afraid they were.

*

The sewer-dwelling rats had been aware of the two-legs' invasion of their territory since the first moment they set foot in the tunnel entrance. They could have attacked and killed them at the start, but one or two might have escaped, alerting others of their kind. They waited and watched to see just how far they would venture. Regarding getting out alive, the two-legs were already past the point of no return. It suited the rats though, allowing the two-legged advance. Each step they took was one less the rats would have to drag the bodies to the deep caves where they kept their food reserve stores. Six fully-grown specimens of the two-legs would feed several new litters of rittens for quite some time.

Many of the rats had already made their way to adjacent tunnels and passageways unknown to the inspection team, effectively blocking their path should they decide to turn back. Surrounded as they were now, the sound of so many of them was coming from both directions, and even through the pipes and fissures. The density of the surrounding rock channelled it even more through the narrowing tunnel section the team had reached. That strange static noise had now become a deafening attack on their senses. Any thoughts about a proper inspection of the tunnels had been abandoned when one of the team made the first murmuring suggestion about 'getting the hell out of here' as he had put it.

Alan was the first to spot them farther ahead in the tunnel: "Look, there, I can see the glints of eyes … and teeth. There must be hundreds of them!"

It was true. In the darkness of the tunnel, the rats' eyes did indeed have a certain glint that shined in stark contrast to the darkness surrounding them. Their teeth too, most the size of a man's thumb like small elephant tusks were intermittently flashing as the light from the men's torches reflected and bounced off their ivory whiteness.

Another of the men instinctively looked back: "Jeez, they're behind us too, just as many. See?"

Again, it was true; a rear-guard of hundreds more had amassed in the opposite direction. They'd all heard the rumours, but none had seen one of the super rats close up so weren't the least bit sure what awaited them. They tried their radios and phones to call for help in the vain hope of getting any kind of signal despite already knowing it would be impossible.

Neither worked. The crew was running out of time … the super rats had abandoned any pretence of stealth in their observations of the two-legs and were slowly approaching them from both directions. The sound of their screeching was getting louder just as those flashing glints in the eye and ivory white reflections of their teeth were becoming noticeably bigger the closer they got.

The only hope the team could cling to was that their sewer inspection clothing was thick and multi-layered so couldn't easily be bitten through. Their boots and gloves were similarly designed to be impervious to bites or tearing. It was only their faces that were left partially exposed, their eye goggles perhaps providing some protection there. The team were hardly confident though …

"I vote we try and fight our way through back

the way we came. If we just wait for them here, we'll be attacked from both sides," Bert said to his colleagues.

"But rats are blocking that way too, we'll still be attacked," one of them suggested.

"I know, but only on the one side."

"But the others … the ones the other way, they'll be coming for us too?"

"That's why we have to make a decision now before they converge on us … is it agreed then, we try and make our way back?" Bert was determined not to just stand and wait for them to attack.

There were sceptical rumblings and whispered murmurs as the other members of the team nodded and thought on it, but really, they knew there was no choice.

The team started their trek back through the tunnel, slowly at first to allow two of them to keep a watch on the rats they hoped to leave behind. The following rats increased their pace in pursuit, quickly shortening the distance between them. The team quickened their own pace, before breaking out into a run. The rats ahead of them remained still, watching the two-legs get closer. The longer and faster the two-legs had to run the more tired they would be when they had to fight was the super rats' thinking. At ten yards though, they too rushed towards them, many leaping at the two-legs head-on. Others swarmed about their lower legs, sinking their teeth into the protective clothing.

The thick material had only been designed to withstand bites from the ground-down teeth of normal rats, not the two and three-inch razor-sharp ones of these. Their claws too had more in common with the talons of a hawk than the short nails of regular species of rat.

The lethal combination made short work of the illusory protection of the team's PPE, quickly bringing them to their knees. Each man was now fighting for his life and would happily have trampled over the fallen bodies of his friends to escape the slaughter. The battle had already been lost though, even before the rear-guard of rats had joined their brothers and sisters in the fray.

The rats had won an easy victory, but Bert and his team had not been like the weak and defenceless ones they met before. They had fought as a team, or at least until they knew they were beaten and panic set in. And they had been strong too, thrashing out with their knives, killing more than a dozen of the super rats in the process. They had not expected such fierce resistance. They also knew the two-legs' failure to return would bring more of their kind, this time ready and better prepared.

The time had come for them to migrate beyond their underground domain. The rats would divide into many smaller mischiefs and spread out in different directions to find and breed with

*

Two hours had now passed the expected time of Bert and his team's return from their inspection. The senior staff in the department were getting worried … *very* worried.

Reports about disappearances of many of Cranberry's homeless were only the tip of the iceberg. There had been others too, world-wide that only the city council were privy to. Cranberry's super-rat filled sewers were just one tiny part of a bigger picture across the world. Rats of all kinds had become a huge problem everywhere, not only their own super-sized ones.

"Get me the National Guard," the Mayor demanded.

*

Even the super rats' enhanced strength and tolerances for all manner of drugs and other substances weren't enough to protect at least half of them from the most toxic poisons the war department had at their considerable disposal. Many thousands were also killed when several detachments of the National Guard flooded their domain with poison gas. When the foggy residue settled, they followed their first two attacks with flame-throwers, incinerating the last few remnants of the super-sized mischief.

The truth about what had occurred in the Cranberry sewers would never be made public, at least not in its entirety. The international community needed time to formulate a defence strategy against the growing problem, unhindered by public panic.

Those who knew the broader picture had good reason to be worried; the whispered rumours of strangely talented rats in England, the secret experiments of Rateznox Genetics, and the countless suppressed reports of rat-related horrors. They all painted a grim picture. War was looming, and nothing could stop it.

*

From their numerous hiding places, the surviving super rats pondered on their recent and first defeat at the hands of the two-legs. They had left it just a single day too late for most of them to escape the two-legs' fury. The attack on them had been swift, and of a size and severity the super rats had not thought possible. They had, of course, fought ferociously in return, killing perhaps hundreds of the uniformed two-legs. But teeth and claws alone had been no match for the terrible weapons the two-legs had used against them. They had had no defence to the strange powders and aromas in the air that burned their lungs and made them die in great pain. And seeing the great spears of hot fire engulfing so many of their number, it was the first time they had felt real fear of their enemy. Clearly, they had under-estimated them, one of the many mistakes they would learn from for the next time.

The surviving super rats remembered the piercing screams that had reverberated throughout the underground network, the memory of which would also stay with the Guardsmen for the rest of their lives just as vividly.

They would replenish their numbers. They would learn from the two-legs. They would fight again … *and win.*

*

It was the first time the super rats had revealed themselves in such numbers and attacked so openly. No one dared believe it would be the last.

***

Rat Farming

There wasn't much that shocked the military police of the Kalamari district, but the scene that greeted them had two of the junior officers throwing up; the stench alone was enough to expel the half-digested contents of even the strongest stomach.

Row after row of the little creatures were hanging by their tales from overhead rails like carcases in a butcher's store-room, only smaller. Pools of blood, way too many to count, were still wet on the drenched floor below where it had drained from their bodies.

Further investigation of the crime scene revealed a host of other equally and more gruesome sights …

*

Norman and Niraz Lewis had run a successful Anglo-Indian restaurant for several years before their latest venture. They had mainly catered for a younger clientele, offering subtle yet appetising combinations of traditional Indian and English dishes. The social mix of London was perfect for them. It wasn't to last.

Following the economic downturn and uncertainty after the UK Brexit vote, one of the first luxuries many of their regular customers had cut back on was eating out. That alone didn't finish them but rather a tightening of food and hygiene regulations following the UK's exit from the EU. The government in their determination to show that this wasn't a carte blanche for the abandonment of regulatory standards had instead drafted a whole new swath of them. It was the mountain of red-tape that had finally killed the Lewis's business.

Rather than try and start again, they packed up and took their business elsewhere.

Niraz still had family and a house and land back in a village in the remote hills of North East India, an area known for its love of the culinary delights of rat recipes.

*

The local Anidi tribe from which Niraz came were an unremarkable and straightforward people. There was one trait that did distinguish them though, and that was their love of rat food. It was a culinary taste shared throughout much of the region. When or how this strange preference had developed had been lost in time. It wasn't due to any scarcity of food, there was an abundance of other local game to be had. Whatever its origins though, Norman and Niraz Lewis had no qualms about exploiting it.

India was so much easier to do business in. It

wasn't that there weren't any regulations to abide by but common sense and a few rupees in the 'right' hand was usually enough to smooth any problems. This was just as well given what the Lewises had in mind. Norman and Niraz were just amazed they hadn't made the move before. Miserable old England could learn a lot from India about doing business, Niraz thought.

The nearby town had proved an excellent location for their new restaurant. Contrary to popular belief, there were plenty of affluent Indians throughout the rural provinces, all eager to spend their new wealth. And the healthy flow of hikers, adventurers, and gap year students passing through the region added to the coffers. What made it profitable though was the abundance of free stock all around – the whole area was swarming with rats. The locals of course, both in Niraz's village and in the town regarded the exquisite rat dishes the couple offered better than any they had ever tasted; the Lewis's culinary expertise was like a breath of fresh air and sophistication.

Not all the Lewis's customers appreciated the sophistication of their menu, or rather wouldn't have done if they had known precisely what they were eating. The Lewis Niraz restaurant was happy to fool its foreign and western clientele into believing the tasty dishes they were being served were exotic varieties of other less controversial meats. And if someone realised or complained, then so what? Norman and Niraz made damned sure it was more profitable for the local officialdom to bury any complaints in bureaucracy than to follow them up

The Lewis's new enterprise was decidedly different from their London one. Yes, catering still played a part but there were several even more unsavoury side-lines to it as well.

*

Until now, the local rat population had accepted their lot in being just another part of the food chain, and the two-legs' mastery and exploitation of them. But a new breed of rat had joined them. They were bigger, stronger, and a whole lot smarter. They had come over on one of the giant container ships from England, and they didn't share their deference to the two-legs.

It wasn't the Anidi's fondness for rat meat that had attracted their attention; they didn't care about their rat-eating tastes. The ancient tribe weren't repulsed by their local rat population, and nor did they try to poison or leave cruel and agonisingly lethal traps for them. Apart from scooping up a relatively few of their number for food, the Anidi were happy to let the rats be and scavenge freely.

Rats had long indulged in bouts of cannibalism

themselves since time began so a few more being similarly lost to the two-legs was nothing exceptional. But what the Lewises were doing was even worse than many of the experiments carried out by Rateznox and other such people and places around the world.

They were still few in number, less than a dozen, but they would soon breed, and with their superior genes would swiftly dominate the local species. Then they would set about putting a stop to the Lewis's wholesale slaughter of their weaker cousins.

Norman Lewis had just returned from the UK after setting up a new export deal. It was one of the last places they had expected to find another market for their products. Niraz greeting him with her news: "We might have a big new order on the books. The only problem we might have is we'll need to import a new species for it, Norman."

"Tell me more, darling."

"China of all places."

"Well, China I can understand. There are many provinces there that still eat them in all manner of ways as snacks or supplements to wider meals. It dates back to the Tang dynasty you know?"

It was just the sort of answer Niraz expected

from a man who never missed an opportunity to show off his well-read education.

"But what new species? They've plenty of their own."

"The order first. They want to know if we can do a spicier version where they're stuffed with honey. I said it shouldn't be a problem with the right preservatives."

"Ah yes. I've heard of that particular dish, used to be very popular with the wealthy nobility, and still is in discreet circles. Could be quite a money-spinner for us. What sort of rat have they specified?"

"One from New Zealand. Rats are a real problem out there, attacking the native wildlife. The government's really cracking down trying to eradicate them, so I'm not sure how easy it will be to get hold of some? The customer wants to import six different varieties, you know, rice and rat, curried rat, rat vegetable dishes, something for everyone. But again, they all have to be made with that particular rat native to New Zealand. Apparently, this species is a highly prized delicacy in some parts of China. I just hope we can get hold of some."

"Ah yes," Norman answered, "the Kiore or Maori Rat as it's also known. Importing some shouldn't be any problem. They're originally from

Polynesia, you know. We can import several breeding pairs from there instead."

"You're so clever, darling, I wouldn't have thought of that."

Their current business was indeed an international one now, with customers in Vietnam, Myanmar, Thailand, the Philippines and Indonesia, Laos, Cambodia, and Ghana, and several others they hoped to add in the future. And with the deal Norman Lewis had just negotiated back in England it had now grown even more profitable.

It wasn't just their abhorrent frozen rat delicacies they dealt in but all sorts of rat-related products – soap from the melted fat of those too old and wretched to provide much meat, and calcium products from the rats' ground-down teeth to name but two, especially popular (and profitable) in the Lewis's far eastern market.

"I forgot to ask, how did things go in miserable old England?" Niraz asked.

"Good. The Nigerians are onboard. They want us to supply ready-made meals for a private club and restaurant they've opened. They're a wealthy lot, but they still want a touch of home and tradition. The giant African rat is a huge favourite with them. We'll need to import a few of them too, but Nigeria to India won't be any problem. And best of all, they're interested in our current range too ... They're eager to add a bit of 'variety and sophistication' to their menus."

*

Within six months, the new breed of rat was dominant throughout the region. The local Anidi and especially some of the lower castes were worried their local rat population might be dying off for some reason. They were unaware that the new breed simply didn't care to be as visible or interact so freely with them ... and nor did they care to be on the Anidi's or any other menu.

It wasn't long before the Lewises too became aware of the seeming reduction in their local rat supply. Much of their workforce came from the local Dalits, one of the poorest castes in all India. In addition to the cursory wage they received from the Lewis's, as was the tradition elsewhere for them, the Dalits harvested some of the smaller rats that plagued the local fields of the wealthy landowners to supplement their diet.

Life as one of India's *Untouchables* wasn't an easy one. The tiny rats the Dalits collected were one of their few pleasures – they were incredibly tender, tasting like chicken or quail. The only unpleasant aspect was the unimaginably awful smell from the rats' burning hair during cooking. It was the tradition to grill them whole so's not to waste any part of the skin or meat, at the same time burning off the hair. The local Anidi and the Dalits were used to and unbothered by it, unlike the Lewises who absolutely hated it whenever they caught the slightest whiff of pungent odour. They had tried persuading them to different ways of preparing the tiny rats, but to no avail. Norman and Niraz had therefore been pleased at first when they were noticing less and less of the repugnant smell about the area.

It was only when reports started coming in of vicious attacks on some of the field hands they became alarmed – employing the Dalits to farm their land was a valuable extra source of income for them. Seeing their usual food source becoming scarcer, many had taken to trying to catch some of the newer and bigger breed of quickly spreading rat. Some had only escaped with nasty bites and scratches, but others had disappeared. Instead of eating the local rat population, they were the ones now being fed upon, nourishing the new breed's many young litters.

The previous trust and respect that had existed between the locals and their rodent neighbours was fast disappearing. That hadn't been the new breed's intention, but they didn't worry about it either. The two-legs had to learn the balance of power was changing. Perhaps some sort of accommodation would return in the future, but it wouldn't be until they had dealt with the Lewis two-legs.

The Lewises had become more security conscious since reports of the new breed of rat swarming the region. They had decided to increase their breeding program within their extensive compound and factory a few miles outside the Anidi village rather than rely on harvesting the local rats. It was there they did most of their rat farming activities, everything from packing and freezing their export dishes to all the other products they derived from the rats' bodies.

With that is mind, they had reinforced the compound perimeter fencing, repairing all the holes and weaknesses in it. Added to this were the numerous traps and poisoned bait they had left. They could have secured it further by electrifying the fencing, but they saw little point in the added expense of that. After all, what was the point? They were just stupid rats at the end of the day even if they were supposedly a bit bigger and stronger.

*

The Lewises had taken a long time to die, longer than the others; the strange new breed of lab rats from England had made sure of that. Over a dozen bodies had been found, the clothes torn and ripped from their naked and mutilated bodies. Most of the flesh had been torn away too, but it was the complete absence of the eyes and genitals that was the most striking … they were a culinary favourite of the rats.

The Kalamari military police weren't even sure they'd ever be able to separate the remains of one body from another for identification, such was the carnage the rats had wrought

A similar scene to that of the Lewis's premises was found at their Nigerian business partners' London premises; rat dishes were definitely off the menu for the foreseeable future.

*

Neither the Dalits nor the village and tribe of the Anidi continued to farm or harvest any kind of rat from that day on.

***

The Return of Ratcula

Ratcula was sitting perched on one of the gothic styled stone statues dotted along the walls of the ancient ruined castle, peering across the wild landscape. There were few humans to be seen, but still one or two were meandering their way across its rugged features and down below in the lush green valley.

The bloodsucking rat had been feeding off them for eight centuries, anonymous and unnoticed. It wasn't so easy now, not these days, not in the cleaner and more affluent parts of the world Ratcula preferred. What with all the CCTV, smartphones, and other seemingly magical technology, the disappearance or unexplained death of even a single one of them aroused attention now.

Life, or rather 'unlife' in Ratcula's case had been so much easier in Queen Victoria's time, provided you stayed clear of the rat catchers that was. Ratcula wondered though how much longer he would have access to such a plentiful supply of food. His mortal cousins of the rodent world had come a long way since the thirteenth century in which Ratcula had been born, much further than would be expected from natural evolution. Side-effects of the humans' pollution and waste had created mortal rats whose strength and speed rivalled his own, rats the size of which he had never seen in all his seven, or was it eight hundred years, he had trouble remembering after so long. More dangerous though were the ones created by the white-coated human scientists, possibly as intelligent and long-lived as himself, ones that didn't need to feed off blood.

That was why Ratcula had come back to England to see for himself this dangerous new rival breed of lab rats.

*

England had changed considerably since he was last there, and even more so since his first arrival all those centuries before. It was the same the world over though, Ratcula lamented.

Ratcula's current travels had taken him to Carreg Cennen castle. It lay Isolated in the rural hinterland of the far western extremes of an area the humans called the Brecon Beacons. It wasn't strictly England of course, but South Wales, not that Ratcula concerned himself with imaginary human borders. It sat atop a fearsome rocky outcrop 300 ft above a sheer drop down into the green valley of the small river Cennen. It was from here the ancient and seemingly immortal rat watched a few lone humans, enjoying their time in the country. And why not? Gone were the vast and wild game filled forests.

Gone too were the wolves and bears that once called them home. The ones that were left were tame and 'people friendly.' The last few corners of the world where the forest demons and devils of the night still held domain had all but disappeared. Ratcula wondered if he was indeed the last of them? He would try and seek out the many he had encountered over the centuries. Some of those he sought he had created himself in his younger days as a newly turned vampire rat.

Ratcula remembered Carreg Cennen castle in all its former glory when the magnificent stone fortress was a worthy home for creatures such as he. Tired of London's squalor after the horror he had inflicted with his bringing of the Black Death, Ratcula had made it his home. There had been an abundance of mice and other small creatures to sustain him between his occasional feasting on human blood.

The human master of the castle had been nothing like the one of Bran castle back in Transylvania, just another mere mortal for all his aristocratic heritage. But like the Master of Bran castle, he did employ a manservant who used ferrets and dogs for the hunting of his kind

Ferrets and dogs no longer worried Ratcula by the time he arrived at Carreg Cennen, or indeed their human masters. But the manservant of the castle had one unusual dog, a monster of a brute whose strength and ferocity Ratcula should have been more respectful of. It was still no match for the demonically powerful rat, but Ratcula sometimes forgot to allow for a creature's greater size when confronted. And so it was when he first encountered the manservant's dog, Samson.

Samson was digging out a mischief of rats in the grounds of the castle, ready for the ferrets to do their work. Ratcula had been with it at the time and was the first to emerge. A single rasp and ungodly hiss were enough for the ferrets to immediately realise this was no earthly rat. Even the manservant's vicious terriers recoiled in fear. Samson was no terrier though, but a monstrous Mastiff the size of a small pony. It stood its ground, bearing its teeth as it stared down at the little rat.

The effect the rat had had had on its other canine friends and even the ferrets was enough for Samson to view the comparatively little rat as a dangerous enemy. Ratcula's mere presence was usually sufficient to deter even the most formidable of foes. But not this time. Samson was a rare breed in that it had not been softened by human contact. It was still a seething bundle of instinct driven fury when it perceived a threat.

Ratcula was fascinated by Samson. It had not

encountered such a ferocious beast in a long time, seeing a touch of the demon in this dog, and even something of itself too. Perhaps it was this almost admiration for the beast that had momentarily dulled Ratcula's senses. Without hesitation, the massive dog had swiped one of its mighty paws in the rat's direction, its talon-like nails extended. The sweeping blow had ripped through Ratcula's fur, tearing into its skin. Sensing victory, Samson leapt upon the little rat, ready to rend its body with his powerful jaws.

Ratcula had not felt such pain in many centuries. The shock of doing so immediately awoke him from the trance-like awe the dog had held him. At that moment, Ratcula too allowed himself to become the purely instinct-driven creature it had once been; pain, fury and that primordial will to survive at all costs saw the little rat transform into something a whole pack of angry Samsons would have been no match for. All Samson found when it set upon the little rat was empty space. Ratcula had instantly leapt a fraction to the side of the dogs' lunging attack. While Samson was still momentarily confused at the rat's seeming disappearance, Ratcula had already used his extraordinary strength to propel himself Samson's almost four feet standing height. His claws had literally speared their way through the dog's fur. He was now firmly anchored in position to sink his impressive retractable razor-sharp fangs deep into the soft, vulnerable flesh of Samson's throat. And sink them he did, giving no thought to the consequences.

Samson had immediately been quietened and immobilised by the paralysing effects by the virus filled saliva that was released whenever Ratcula fully retracted his fangs. It was only necessary to fully withdraw them if he wanted to 'turn' a creature. Usually, Ratcula only retracted them sufficiently to take enough blood to replenish his strength. Right now, he was gorging on his prey like the proverbial condemned man feasting on his last meal. With so much of the vampire virus now in Samson's bloodstream, its fate could only go one of two ways. It would either survive and live through the centuries or die within the next few minutes while the vampire rat drained Samson's blood beyond the point of recovery.

Ratcula could barely remember when he had last fed so well. The life-force in this one was as strong as any he had ever tasted. The frenzied anger and fury that had overwhelmed the demonic little rat was starting to subside. It still wasn't too late to pull back from the brink and allow the dog to live. Ratcula wondered though if it might be some small mercy to put Samson out of his misery?

Immortality had been something the two-legs had sought throughout the ages. But for nature's smaller creatures, ones such as Ratcula where even a normal span of life could be a day to day struggle, it could be as much a burden as it was a blessing ...

Did he have the right to inflict that same burden on another? Then he thought on his own life; it had been hard in the early days but looking back, he had and still continued to enjoy a wonderfully long life. He enjoyed too the wisdom that came with each passing century, and all the other 'abilities' that being a vampire creature bestowed. Above all, he had never regretted his own 'turning' by the two-legged Master all those centuries past.

Ratcula withdrew his blood-soaked fangs from Samson's throat. It would not be easy for the giant dog to survive the centuries unnoticed the way he did. Samson was too big to live in plain sight among others of his kind. Nor were there any sewers or hidden places in the hollow walls of the two-legs' houses, basements, cellars, and other such places for a creature the size of Samson to hide and make a home. But Samson would have advantages too. A beast his size would be proportionally stronger, faster, and more powerful, way more so than a tiny creature the size of Ratcula.

It was only now that Ratcula considered just what it was he might be creating. A creature already as large and formidable as Samson would be a terrifying demon now that it had been 'turned.'

By now, the human two-legged one's manservant and his menagerie of terriers and ferrets had long fled the scene. The thunderous storm raging through the valley was probably part of the reason for that, not that Ratcula was concerned either way.

It was several more hours before Samson awoke a very different creature from its previous mortal self. Its wild instinct was now rivalled by a swath of knowledge and the beginnings of understanding.

The torrential rain combined with the sound and sight of lightning assaulting the surrounding landscape would once have sent Samson scampering for shelter. Such storms were one of the few things that would once have induced fear in the great beast just as it would with Ratcula before his own turning. Strangely though, Samson remained calm and indifferent to it.

Ratcula had eyed the newly created vampire creature with caution. This was no longer just some mortal dog the rat's demonic abilities could easily dispatch to the afterlife. Samson was now every bit Ratcula's equal, and given its greater size, its superior too. Nonetheless, Ratcula stood his ground. He knew from his own experience, Samson would be confused and have many questions about what had happened to him. And like the two-legged Master had been at the time, Ratcula would be the one to answer those questions.

"You've done this to me," were Samson's first thoughts. Ratcula heard them clearly.

"I knew you were different the moment you hissed. The others knew it too. And now I'm different … the same as you?"

"Not quite the same. It's different for each of us, even for creatures of the same kind. What it will mean for you only time will tell. But you will have a lot of that. We don't get old and die like other animals or the two-legs."

Their conversations went on long into the night. Ratcula explained what being a vampire creature would mean for Samson just as the two-legs Master had done with him: the danger of accidentally 'turning' those you fed on, the strange abilities the dog would soon develop like telepathy, strength and speed, and the heightened senses.

"How many others? Like us, I mean?" Samson asked.

"I don't know, not exactly. There's a few I've turned over the years. And I know some of the two-legged kind have turned dogs such as you for loyal companionship down the centuries … though I don't know how many two-leg vampires still exist, perhaps none. Most have been hunted down and killed over the past two centuries.

"We can live indefinitely but we can also be killed too, it's important to remember that."

Samson pondered the little rat's answers to his many questions. He had understood the answers better and quicker than Ratcula had thought, probably due to his greater natural intelligence before the turning.

"And now? What happens?"

"Anything you want. You're free to stay or go as you like, freer than you've ever been."

Ratcula already suspected Samson's intentions. He may have been turned, but his loyalty to his Master, that special bond that exists between dogs and their human masters would persist until the two-legs died. Samson would remain with him in the castle until old age took the mortal one of the pair.

"You're right, I will be staying. But you must go. You've already revealed yourself to be more than you are. My Master is old and no longer strong. It won't arouse suspicion when I outlive him. After that, well, I can decide then."

What had happened with Ratcula and Samson had all been some two hundred years before

Ratcula's return to the UK. Ratcula wondered what had become of Samson. After so long a life he was lonely for another of his kind. That was why he chose the ruins of the castle as the first stop on his return. Was Samson still alive, somewhere nearby? The demonic rat allowed his heightened senses to reach out in all directions, searching for some feeling of him. After a few days, he had to conclude Samson was either dead or had moved on to new territories. He hoped it was the latter.

It came as a surprise then when the beastly dog approached him. Ratcula had been feeding on some small animal when Samson appeared. Feeding was one of the few times when a vampire creature wasn't fully aware of every sight and sound about them. It was less than a mile from where the two had first encountered one another shortly before Ratcula had turned him.

"So, you've returned?" was all Samson thought to the rat. Ratcula was pleased at his sight, though he detected no sense of the same in Samson, just a mild curiosity. Still, that was better than anger or rage – for all his vampire strength and speed, he would have been no match for the demonic dog had it wanted to kill him.

The two eyed one another. Whatever Samson's lack of feeling towards the little rat, they were both creatures of another world most of the two-legs never knew or even suspected might exist. There was a bond between them neither could deny; it was part of what prompted Ratcula's return and Samson to emerge from the dark, vast cavernous world beneath the wild landscape of the Brecon Beacons.

"I wondered if you'd return here. I sensed your return many weeks ago when you first stepped off the container ship." Samson's thoughts surprised Ratcula. It was clear the other vampire creature's abilities far exceeded his own … was that down to its natural greater size and intelligence, like that of the Master back in Transylvania?

"I enjoyed my years here. It was a magnificent castle and fine place to shelter."

"There's little left of the original castle, just the surface ruins the humans sometimes visit. There's still many of the old hidden tunnels though, and I've dug more, connecting them with my own world."

"You never wanted to leave, explore the world out there?"

"It's not so simple for one my size. I can't sneak aboard the humans' great ships so easily as you. I've prowled their cities at night though, seen much of this island of theirs. But as you told me all those years ago, time is different for us. I'll see more of the human world when it suits me or when there's no more feeding to be had in these parts."

"It's been good to see you again, Samson. It worried me, turning you as I did, whether or not it would be a gift or a curse?"

"I enjoy my life now so it needn't trouble you." It pleased Ratcula to know he hadn't been wrong in creating another of his kind. There were so few of them left now. Perhaps he would turn others again, maybe even some humans.

"I may see you here again one day ... or some other place. But now it's time for me to leave."

"To seek out those others?" The question intrigued Ratcula. He knew Samson didn't mean others like themselves.

"Others of what you used to be, only stronger, faster, the ones the humans created. There are many of them now."

"You know of them?"

"Yes. They share many of our abilities. I don't know if they can live as long, but they live much longer than ordinary mortal creatures. There was a mischief of them nearby, but they moved on. I don't know where. I can't sense them as I can others of *our* kind."

"There'll be more of them in the cities I would think. I'll go to London to seek them out."

"They're not as strong or fast as you, but their numbers are many and growing each day. You may be a rat, but you're not one of them so be careful, they may turn on you." Ratcula nodded his appreciation, not just for the warning but the show of concern.

*

It amazed Ratcula just how much London had changed since the last time he was there. Much of it was so clean and sterile now, filled with gleaming shiny towers reaching to the sky. But for those of Ratcula's diminutive size, they spent their lives eye-level with the dark and squalid side of the great city. It was rare for the little rat to be more than a few feet from a drain or sewage pipe, some entrance to the subterranean world much of the city's vermin called home.

Ratcula was prowling the same streets he once did over two centuries before. He'd lived through the fearful years of his mortal kind's nemesis, Jack Black, the Royal Rat Catcher, and decades later while hunting for food, had witnessed one of Jack the Ripper's brutal murders. The human two-legs had possessed a savagery he'd rarely seen even among the most frenzied feeding rages of a vampire creature.

When the human killer was done, Ratcula had taken the opportunity to enjoy his share of the unfortunate woman's life, practically bathing in the blood-drenched aftermath of the gruesome slaying. It was a rare pleasure for Ratcula being able to feed so generously from one of the two-legs, usually having to restrict itself to just a small sampling for fear of killing or turning his human host.

The little rat was pleased to see that despite the superficial advances the city had made, there was still a sizeable number of the less fortunate two-legs strewn about the streets and districts; Ratcula would continue to have his pick of them to feed off.

It was while creeping along a water-pipe, eying the mass of homeless two-legs huddled along the Thames embankment, Ratcula observed a small group of rats sidled alongside one of them. They had already decided on *their* prey for the night. It was the smell of so much blood spilt about the ground that had first attracted Ratcula's attention to them – so negligent, he thought, allowing so much to go to waste. He was inclined to approach and wrest the meal from them. Had they been ordinary rats, mortal ones like he had once been, that's what he would have done. They were different though - not different like himself, but some human science made abominations. Since his return to London, he had avoided much contact with the native rats. The few that he had encountered still showed the same deference most mortal creatures had always done. There were a few that did not though, instead treating him with indifference or suspicion. It was a reaction the vampire creature had never felt from other rats before.

The rats huddling about the dead two-legs were unafraid when they became aware of Ratcula's presence, turning to face him. It should not have been possible, but Ratcula could hear their thoughts just like they were other vampire creatures or a human – but they were neither, and nor should they have even had the capacity to form complex language-based thoughts.

"You're not from the lab or one of us. What are you?" was what they were asking, knowing this other rat could hear their thoughts. There was no fear, no deference about them. Ratcula assumed they would be able to 'hear' his own thoughts in return.

"No. I'm different from you, but we have more in common than separates us." The mortal rats approached him, cautiously, sensing that this other kind of rat might still be a danger to them despite being alone.

"You are right to be wary of me. Even outnumbering me, we would be evenly matched."

They halted their approach, sensing the truth of that. There was no lying in such communication.

"You're a blood creature, aren't you? We've met others like you, but never one of our own form?"

"So that's what you call us? Here in London? These others, what form did they take?"

"Dog, cats, wolves. Even some two-legs of your kind. Many others too, scattered far and wide." Ratcula tried to look further into their minds to learn more about them. It was to be one of the rare times Ratcula was reminded of the limits to his abilities; collectively, the lab rats were able to close their minds to him, shutting him out as easily as a two-legs vampire might.

"I've no quarrel with you. I'm no friend of the two-legs either," Ratcula told them, "look into my own mind and see ..." and look they did.

They saw Ratcula's own siblings slaughtered by the manservant's dogs and ferrets all those centuries back, and the burning hatred he had felt. They were impressed too with the many millions of the two-legs the rat-like blood creature had killed in revenge with its bringing of the Black Death. Ratcula was no immediate threat to them, not yet. But what if there were many more such blood creatures? These blood creatures needed the two-legs as a blood source.

Would these blood creatures ally themselves with their mortal cousins or serve the blood lusting two-legged ones of their kind?

Better to kill them all, they thought. These others had no intention of sharing their ownership of the world once the humans were gone. They could have hidden their thoughts from Ratcula, but they didn't. Clearly, they considered one lone vampire rat no threat to them either now or in the future. Ratcula, on the other hand, chose not to share his own thoughts; though their complete lack of fear was alarming, it also demonstrated their over-confidence. Ratcula and others of his kind had walked the earth for thousands of years – these test-tube creations of the two-legs' would do better not underestimating such an enemy.

Ratcula sensed the rats were summoning others of their kind to join them, too many for him to fight. He was about to take flight when he sensed another presence. This was one of his *own* kind, and stronger, one he recognised …

Even as Ratcula now realised who had come to his aid, Samson was already leaping from behind and over him, landing right amongst the rival group of rats and their prey. With a single swipe of his paw, he sent several of them in all directions while tearing into more of them with his powerful jaws and canine fangs. His thunderous growl as he attacked was likely to attract attention, and so he ended the battle swiftly. They had tried to subdue the new and more dangerous blood creature by sheer weight of numbers but were powerless to fight such ferocity. Again, they had underestimated their enemy, or perhaps, were merely over-confident in their own newfound strength and abilities. What was better was that Samson had left none alive to warn any others of their mistake.

"I was curious as to what you had in mind with these other rats. I thought you might be considering joining or even leading them?"

"And you were going to stop me, was that it?"

"Yes. But I see I was wrong. These creations of the humans are as much a threat to you as to the humans, and even to us. It may not be possible to prevent their war with the humans but we need to think about our own survival, and at least minimising the human death-toll."

"Ah, yes, I keep forgetting that 'man's best friend' bond you have with them."

"That's nothing to do with it. I just prefer the taste of their blood sometimes. I don't want to go hungry or be forced to feed off smaller creatures, they don't nourish me the same way."

*

The two vampire creatures could see the coming war. They both doubted the two-legs' capacity to fight it, not with so many differently enhanced rats. Ratcula had already realised these mutant rivals would see vampire creatures as a threat to their dominance. His own kind were few in number compared to the growing number of enhanced lab rats and the super breeds from the sewers. Nor did he know what other monstrous super strains had been created in other Rateznox laboratories around the world. And then there was the giant Sumatran spawning those ones hidden away in the secret labyrinth of tunnels beneath the city.

Ratcula wondered if perhaps it was time to reintroduce more demons to the world, others of their own kind and even two-legged ones to lead any fight with the mutant rats?

Samson was of a similar mind. They would need soldiers and allies to fight these mutant abominations ...

***

Rats on the radio?

News Views Radio on 125 FM, or NVR as it was usually shortened to, was the most popular radio station in the county. It followed a similar format to many other such stations. They would get various experts into their studio to discuss some local news item and then invite callers to ring in to ask questions, express their own opinions, or just have their say on the matter. The current topic was pest control and the increasing problem of rats running around the streets and among the garbage bags left out for collection.

Rick Collins was today's 'expert,' explaining to the controversial radio host, Josh 'Gobby' Galloway, just what clean and lovely creatures rats really were. Gobby of course, in line with the general tone of his show, was having none of it …

"I'm sorry, Rick, but I just don't agree. Rats are nothing but filthy disease-ridden vermin."

"That's really quite wrong. It's just their being forced to live in the sewers and other similarly unsanitary conditions, their large numbers, and having to scavenge for food among the garbage that gives them that reputation."

"But you don't deny they're disease carriers?

You only have to think of the Black Death. That was spread by rats, wasn't it?"

"Another misconception, Mr Galloway!" Rick Collins snapped. "It wasn't the rats themselves that spread the plague, but the fleas they were infested with, *they* were the culprits in that particular case."

"So. The fleas were diseased then, but the rats *carried* the fleas, ergo the rats carried the disease!" 'Gobby' Galloway snapped back.

Josh 'Gobby' Galloway was a past master at twisting the words of his guests in the pursuit of controversy, or when it suited him, simply to be argumentative. He knew the public's general revulsion of rats, so it followed that it wouldn't have done his popularity any good to be heard agreeing with some 'expert' defending them.

"This is Josh Gobby Galloway broadcasting on NVR 1225FM bringing you the best in live radio debate. Let's take our first caller, please, and it's Leanne Michaels from our very own good ol' town of Witchitar, go ahead my dear …"

"Thank you. Josh. The way I see it, we should be culling them like we do other vermin when there's too many of them, or they become a problem. Where I live you can see them running around the town quite openly, especially on the night before garbage

collection days when people put out their bags. They tear holes in them and rummage through the contents, and when the garbage men collect the bags, because of the holes, some of it falls out and is left on the streets. It's just not good enough."

"Thank you for that, Leanne … over to you, Rick, is a rat cull the answer?"

"No, of course it's not. The problem lies in our town planning and the way we organise our garbage collections. Get that right, and the problems Leanne highlights will take of themselves. And might I add, the sort of culling suggested here simply isn't possible, there's just too many of them spread across too many locations."

"We have another caller, Russ from Denby. What's your take on the rat problem, Russ?"

"Horrible … BLEEP … they are."

"Easy there, Russ, you'll get us in strife with the broadcasting watchdogs with language like that," Josh interrupted. "But I know what you mean, go on …"

"Yeah, sorry about that, but seriously, I can't believe Rick saying we can't kill the little, I mean rats, because there's too many, that's just stupid. It's like saying ya can't execute murderers 'cos they might

kill us."

"I'm sorry, I don't see the point you're making there, erm, Russ was it?" Rick replied.

"Saying we can't kill the rats because there's too many of them. Isn't that the reason we need to kill them because there are too many?"

"He has a point there, Rick," Josh agreed.

Rick shrugged his shoulders and sighed, realising he'd been sandbagged into what was little more than a daytime entertainment show rather than a serious discussion.

*

Like many country farm and ranch houses in the American mid-west, this latest one they had reached was primarily made of wood. The wooden structure would be no match for the thousands of grotesque teeth and claws tearing it away splinter by splinter. They had already had their fill of the cows and other animals about the farm, including the two young farm-hands. But there were still many young rittens waiting to be fed, and any other two-legs inside would add to their meal. They would need the extra food for the migration to the nearest city.

*

There were several more calls with listeners urging

more should be done about the increasing rat problem. Despite the secrecy surrounding events of a rat related incident in the town of Cranberry about 50 kilometres away, rumours were rife. Several callers had expressed their fears of being similarly attacked. It was perhaps why the next caller wasn't taken as seriously as she should have been …

"We have another caller on the line, I think she said Mandy Jenkins from … Sorry, could you say again, there's a strange crackle on the line …"

"I'm at home on my farm, about 15 miles outside Witchitar, and I need help. They're everywhere … everywhere I tell you!"

Another nutjob caller, Josh 'Gobby' Galloway thought, immediately seeing the opportunity to liven up the show even more.

"What are everywhere? Are you talking about rats, or maybe aliens? Or is it something else?"

"Oh for … the woman's clearly distressed by something," Rick snapped at the radio host, partly because of the way he'd been treated by Josh himself.

"It's the rats!" Mandy screamed again, *"They're all around the house, in the barn, and they're trying to get in …"*

"And how many rats are we talking about here,

Mandy? Surely not enough to get all excited about, but if they're really bothering you, do what my old ma used to and take a broom to them, knock the little brutes …" A stern grimace and gesturing motion of a hand cutting across a throat from Josh's boss was enough to halt the radio host's flippant reply. Mandy continued:

"I tried calling 911 … there's just …. So many … they … they're getting louder …"

Much of the what Mandy was saying was inaudible due to what sounded like a bad line. Usually, Josh would have just cut her off and moved onto the next caller, but her mad ramblings were bound to keep his audience listening.

"It sounds like you've got quite a problem there, Mandy … and it's not even garbage day," Josh quipped again, deciding to ignore his boss's urging to go easy on the caller.

"What did the 911 operator tell you, Mandy? Whatever it was, you need to call them again, insist on them sending someone out to you," Rick interjected. He didn't believe her story about being besieged by rats, but she definitely needed some sort of help.

"They're on their way … they couldn't say how long it would be … I need help now."

The radio staff apart from Josh were all as concerned as Rick. Perhaps she was a nutjob as Josh thought, but they recognised it was real fear and panic in the caller's voice.

"Oh God! ... They're in the ... everywh ... pleaseeeee ... help m ..."

There was just crackle and hissing on the line now, like before only louder.

"Mandy, please, we'll get you help," Rick was telling her, "we'll trace your number and get you help, just hang on," he urged again, hoping she was still listening.

And then the line went dead. It had been the strangest call the station had ever received. Along with the rest of the broadcast team, even Josh 'Gobby' Galloway hoped and prayed it was some sort of bizarre hoax or the paranoid ramblings of an attention seeking nutjob just as he had first thought.

*

The two state patrol officers sent to answer Mandy Jenkins' call had been diverted by another call from their control point. The woman Mandy had originally spoken to during her 911 call had tried to phone her back to see if she still needed assistance. The line was completely dead, so she had upgraded the original call to top priority. When the two officers did finally arrive, they were already stressed from almost being run off the road. That paled in comparison though to what they found at Mandy Jenkins' farm. What little was left of Mandy's body was still clutching the phone she had used to call the radio station. Apart from that, what was left was barely recognisable as a person.

Immediately suspecting some sort of criminal homicide, they had called for backup. The other bodies were discovered in a similar state, both livestock and human alike. Forensics had determined rats to be the cause, which given the number of rat droppings all about the place, came as no surprise.

The only addition to the patrol officers' report was about them spotting a swarm of something, well they didn't know what exactly, scurrying across the state-highway, forcing the two officers to swerve to avoid them.

*

The staff at NVR weren't to know at the time, but the crackling and hissing noise they thought was interference on the line during Mandy's call was really a combination of hundreds of rats scratching and gnawing outside and at the telephone cables.

The escaped super rats from the Cranberry sewers incident knew they would attract attention if they didn't disperse and spread out. Half their number had come to the city, mostly taking up residence in the sewer network below the streets of Witchitar. The super rats had learnt from their mistake of concentrating all their forces in the one area and would not do so again.

Many had taken to living among the two-legs themselves in their houses, basements, and in the crawl spaces beneath many of their other buildings. They hid in plain sight among their urban cousins already there. When any were spotted, they were just thought of as being exceptionally large, a trick of the light, or were mistaken for some bigger creature like a cat or a dog.

The super rats quickly dominated the smaller and weaker species of their kind. Interbreeding with their smaller cousins was producing bigger and stronger new litters of rittens; the effects of the hormone and steroid filled meat was being passed on to new generations, fast replenishing the super rat numbers. More and more of those that had taken refuge in the town sewers were emerging to join them as their numbers also multiplied.

For the inhabitants of Witchitar, the old adage about never being more than six feet away from the nearest rat was now chillingly accurate. Would the National Guard be willing or even able to use their deadly toxins, poisoned gas, and flame-throwers against them now they were resident among the two-legs themselves?

Three months later ...

For the past couple of days, NVR 125FM had been experiencing some difficulties with their phone-in shows. A sort of hissing and buzzing sound on the line during some of the calls. It wasn't serious at first, just the odd crackle they sometimes got in the hot weather, overheating of the wires was the engineers' usual stock excuse for it.

If anyone had had reason to visit the dis-used storage basement of the NVR building they would have noticed it was much louder down there, even before they got through the door.

Everyone had pretty much forgotten about Mandy's call until now. A junior member of the staff had casually remarked how similar that strange crackle on the line back then was to what they were hearing with their current caller.

And then the line went dead ... but not the strange crackling noise, that continued ... getting louder ... and closer ...

It was the last time NVR 125FM ever broadcast.

***

Raticide

Unbeknown to anyone outside the Rateznox Genetics' Board and those working in it, Rateznox had what they called Department 'D.' It was the corporate equivalent of a Black Ops section, that part of the company which oversaw all their special projects, the ones they hid from international scrutiny. Unfortunately, many of their laboratories and rogue researchers were as indifferent to Rateznox's supervision as was Rateznox was to that of the international scientific community. It was why the genetics company had been plagued by one crisis after another, each time only surviving the consequences more by luck than design. Their luck was running out …

The World Health Organisation was debating what to do about the increasing rodent problem and the global health issues it was causing. Rats, mice, and other assorted vermin were seen as a blight on the West's gleaming skyscraper image. What they should have been debating was their own reluctance to compel their respective governments to invest properly in infrastructure, reliable waste collection, and proper sanitation. Instead, they turned to Rateznox Genetics to solve their problem. It was a fortuitous choice – it was Rateznox who was responsible for the current problem, a project they had embarked up some three years prior … they were now poised to reap the supposed benefits …

*

Someone in Rateznox had come up with the bright idea of creating poison and disease resistant rats and then being the ones to come up with a solution to them. It was hardly the most original idea anyone ever had, but it was still a potential Rateznox money spinner - and a possible solution to another of Rateznox's problems.

The only sane voice of opposition to the idea had been Dr Natalie Martins ….

"So far, gentlemen, we've avoided international condemnation and closure for our past … how shall I put it? 'Mishaps,' for want of a better word? Need I remind you all, each and every last one of us would be languishing in a prison cell if the full truth of the HN247 problem had come to light? Do we really want to embark on another such venture?"

"That as may be, Dr Martins, but it didn't, and we're not. What *has* happened though is the emergence of public resistance and distrust of pharmaceutical and GM products. That has hit our share price hard. We need new revenue sources if we're to continue in business. If you can't overcome your ethical concerns, perhaps you need to rethink your position in the company?"

There was nothing Dr Natalie Martins would have liked more than to call their bluff, telling the Rateznox Board precisely what they could do with their job. But turning her back on a problem wasn't in her nature. She could only exercise some control and sanity in Rateznox's plans from the inside. And there was another more immediate problem – apart from being too valuable an asset to lose to some rival company – they would never allow that – she knew too many of Rateznox Genetics' failures. Rateznox's chief bio-geneticist doubted she'd live to reach the door if she tried resigning.

"I tell you, I don't like it, "Natalie Martins was telling Mark, her fellow bio-geneticist, "there are good reasons why this sort of research and experiments are globally banned. It will take just one mistake to bring on a catastrophe that will trivialise the board's worries about bloody stock prices."

"Then why complete the work? Tell them you've hit a dead-end with it."

"What they want isn't that difficult, just dangerous. There are at least a dozen other scientists who could complete it, including you."

"But none of us are as good as you, the board

knows that." Natalie smiled. She thought for a moment there might be a tinge of flattery in that last remark, knowing how Mark felt about her. She quickly dismissed the idea; when it came to work, he was every bit the professional as herself.

Natalie Martins' lab wasn't the one working on the project; hers was leading it but Rateznox Genetics was passing on her results to others around the world, places that took a more relaxed view of ethics and safety protocols. As always, Rateznox was taking dangerous short-cuts in the science behind the intended immunities for their rats. They weren't engineering rodent immunity as such, just 'borrowing' it from other species. Disease and toxin-resistant genes from numerous different animals were being spliced into the rats' DNA, but not before modifying them to be susceptible to one specific deadly life-destroying cocktail of Rateznox's making, RN249. Both sides of the ill-advised project were recipes for another of Rateznox's genetic disasters.

Thousands of Rateznox Genetics' modified rats were eventually released into the wild from their far eastern laboratory breeding centres. They knew the rats would breed and quickly pass on their artificially spliced in immunities, eventually finding their way aboard the giant trade tankers en route to the west. They considered releasing equal numbers there too but decided against it. There was too much scrutiny, too many suspicious eyes on them there

It had been designated a long-term project, five years they had estimated. As it was, the WHO had learnt from their past mistakes, unlike Rateznox Genetics, in taking a mere three years to address Rateznox's engineered rat problem.

Despite almost half the world's rat population were carrying the disease and toxin-resistant genes, it wasn't the numbers Rateznox had hoped for. Even so, they remained on target to meet their projected profits forecasts and proceeded with stage two of the RN249 project.

Despite their total ineffectiveness, sales of rat poisons had initially sky-rocketed across the board in the public's last-ditch efforts to drive them from their homes and streets. Rateznox had made a short-term killing as did anyone who had a rodent pest product on the market. When nothing worked, those sales dropped just as dramatically. Only Rateznox Genetics was unconcerned by this, it was their cue, albeit a little prematurely, to implement the second part of their plan.

*

"... After extensive research, Rateznox Genetics is happy to announce the successful completion of the

RN249 trials since being tasked by the WHO in helping them with the widely publicised supposed disease and poison resistant super rats. The public can rest assured we are confident our new pest control product will once and for all put an end to this scourge on our streets."

Dr Natalie Martins switched off the TV news announcement. She had known it was coming, just not the knight in shining armour tone of it – Rateznox Genetics was anything but.

"Can you believe that? They're laying the groundwork to be hailed as the fucking heroes of the hour for a problem they created in the first place … again!"

Dr Natalie Martins cursed herself for ever having gone along with the insane plan. She knew she'd had no choice, not really, but she of all people knew the dangers and possible consequences of what they were doing. She should have at least tried to do more to stop the madness, no matter what.

"Don't blame yourself, honey. At least with you leading the project, there's some chance it won't blow up in their faces," Mark tried to reassure her.

"In *our* faces too," she corrected him. "Do you think for one minute our lords and masters will quietly sit back and accept responsibility when they can wheel us out as the mad rogue scientists? We make easier and better monsters for the public to hate than shadowy men in suits."

"What exactly is it you're afraid might happen, Natalie? I mean, creating drug and disease resistant rats and then dealing with it … It's hardly ethical, but you talk about it as if it's the end of the world?" She paused at his question, pondering on Mark's last words there … *the end of the world*? If he only he knew, she thought, but of course he didn't. Natalie hadn't told him just how far she had gone to create what Rateznox had demanded of her. She still trembled when she thought of the monstrous mutations their initial gene splicing had created – rats with six legs, rudimentary wings, even antennae instead of regular whiskers. Rateznox had wanted to keep them alive for further experiments just for the sake of it. But such creatures were never meant to be, and she had urged for them to be destroyed. She hoped they had? She wondered though how many more such mutant genes were now lying dormant in subsequent litters of their experiments, waiting to escape among their wild offspring? She put the thought out of her mind, it was too frightening to contemplate.

"Natalie? You okay?" Mark asked, concerned by the distant look in her eyes. The sound of his voice and a gentle nudge of her arm snapped Natalie out of her morbid speculations.

"Oh, I'm sorry. I was just thinking … miles away I guess."

Mark smiled, replying, "Yeah, I could see that." She went on to tell him of the true extent of her fears, and of the mutant rats from their first experiments and of even more hideous hybrids rumoured to have been created in the far eastern labs, all based on her research. Mark could barely believe what she was telling him. He hadn't known any of it, not even suspected. She had gone behind his back to get him assigned to a less controversial project, hoping to shield him from the inevitable fall-out should things go wrong.

Across the world, every means of administering Rateznox's latest product was employed. Being harmless to humans and most animals other than those harbouring Rateznox's modified genes, it had been carried in the water supplies, foods the rats were particularly fond of, and every rat pest product still on the market.

It was the urban populations that hated rats the most. They saw them as a sign of filth and poverty, especially when seeing them scurrying about the drains and gutters, and everywhere else the humans considered dirty. It was mainly there the effects of Rateznox's latest rat-ridding product were to be observed. So many were dying, their bodies were being rounded up in their tens of thousands daily. Even with their smaller size, such were the numbers they were having to be dumped in newly and hastily created land-fill sites on the outskirts of the towns and cities

Amid the mountain high heaps of gene-modified rat corpses, there was movement, only slight, but it was there. A small rat was edging its way through the putrefying remains of its brothers and sisters. The crisp nauseating smell of burnt fur and flesh filled its nostrils from where the two-legs had turned their flame-throwers to set the dead bodies ablaze. But even wave after wave of the of the burning fire hadn't been enough to scorch them all.

For every thousand that had died, one or two would emerge unscathed by either fire or the RN249 rat killing cocktail. Nature itself was weeding out the human created abominations but not all. Never one to miss a new evolutionary opportunity, it allowed a small percentage to survive. Amid the rodent genocide that Rateznox Genetics intended to take credit for, a new strain was emerging to reclaim their place in the grand scheme of life. But it would not be as before. They had no intention of suffering such losses again. In one respect, Mother Nature and the rats were of one mind – Man's status as the dominant species and position at the top of the food chain should not continue.

*

With their numbers decimated, the rats had paid a heavy price, but the survivors had a new weapon at their disposal – they were now impervious to whatever poisons the two-legs could throw at them. They had many new allies too – the freak mutants, the giant ones of the sewers, the super strong and aggressive ones across the endless water, and of course, the strangely gifted ones that had escaped from one of Rateznox's British based labs and even spread to the shores of India.

They would breed like never before. They would pass on that new trait and many others to their countless offspring. And then ...*They would return* ...

Epilogue

Confidential Report from Section 'D' (Extract)

Dr Natalie Martins was reading an extract of a report she had received anonymously. It was heavily abbreviated but enough to alarm her. The fact it been passed onto her at all suggested she wasn't alone in her fears. What worried more was what was missing from it?

While the monetary rewards and increases in the Rateznox share price should not be downplayed, we cannot assume it to be a complete success. As we all know, this was never about our financial status. Forty-five per cent of the world's rat population still remained free of the resistant genes at the time we were forced to act, mostly those in the wild rather than urban centres of population. We cannot, therefore, be confident of having exterminated the cognitively and otherwise enhanced strain known to have escaped our UK based facility, also suspected of having spread to the Kalamari province of Northern India. We should, therefore, continue to monitor world-wide any reports of unusual rodent related activity. Only time will tell ...

***

King Rat

There are few sights in nature or the supernatural that's grotesque appearance can compare with that of a King Rat. Even the mythical faces of Medusa would be easier on the eye, for having been turned to stone upon their look, you would not have to continually suffer the nightmare image of having seen them.

Tales of King Rats had been around for as long as anyone could remember, passed from one generation to the next among the peoples of Eastern Europe. They were spoken of in hushed and fearful tones, and as being bad omens and bringers of bad luck.

The exact origins or just when the stories of a giant entwined mass of rats first emerged had faded into mystery and mythology, but they could be traced to the middle ages and the plague of the Black Death. Many believed they went back even further, and wise village elders would tell stories of them to frighten and stir the imaginations of their little ones.

Of course, such stories had long since been dismissed as superstitious nonsense in a modern and more enlightened world. Anything that was out of sight, as most often a King Rat was, inevitably became a case of out of mind too, and so, such stories became just that – stories. But amid the explosive growth of the rat population, sightings and further tales of these obscenities on the eye were again being reported, and however bizarre the telling, there was good reason to believe them …

The creature meandering its way around the extensive network of abandoned tunnels beneath the streets of London knew nothing of the King Rat legends. And yet, it was the exact modern equivalent. It was something worse than all the Rateznox hybrid monstrosities put together, a pure rat mutation, encapsulating every horrid and vile trait of the species, and many more besides.

In its early days, London's very own home-grown King Rat, or the giant one as it was called back then, was a hideous mutation brought about by one of the Rateznox Genetics' ill-advised concoctions, a serum containing cells and DNA from the legendary giant rat of Sumatra. The Sumatran creature was another of nature's equally hideous and disease-ridden monsters, though not an actual King Rat as such.

The London laboratory induced creation had grown to even more monstrous proportions since then, amassing the minions that would scurry about its feet and body, tending and caring for it like soldier ants attending their queen. And the analogy doesn't end there. The King Rats of old were nothing in comparison to this modern reincarnation of the ancient folklore, minuscule even. They usually consisted of anywhere from just a few up to about 30 or so rats. Their tails would be horribly tangled and entwined, made impossible to separate by years of congealed sweat or even worse unmentionable substances.

A similar thing had happened with the creature now hiding beneath the ground, but like the queen of the ant colony, this one had thousands in attendance. Its 50-foot-long tail was the central strand that bound it with those of a thousand more, the body of the new King Rat sitting atop and riding its legion of subordinate rats like a chariot. And it was not only their tails that bound them together in their unnatural fusion but their minds too, a hive-like shared consciousness enabling the seemingly conjoined mischief to think and act as one.

"Look, Sam, we can't just dismiss the eye-witness accounts of more than a dozen passengers as a mass hallucination," train driver Dean Richardson was telling the regional manager of the Central line, that part of the network where the tunnels ran deepest below the heart of the city.

"I'm not trying to, but you've got to admit, we should at least try to look for a more rational explanation," he replied, anxious not to say anything that might give any credence to the reports. It was bad enough having to fend off media ridicule of leaves or the wrong kind of rain or snow without now having to explain of monsters on the line.

"Yes, we should, just as you should be willing to admit that dozens of people seeing the same thing can't all be wrong."

Dean had been the first to be confronted by several terrified passengers when he had pulled into the next station. Dean hadn't seen the alleged creature himself as he had been concentrating on looking forward, but the passenger accounts were all surprisingly consistent. Whatever it was, it had appeared to them as the train passed an old disused station and branch tunnel, also no longer an active part of the network. The few brief seconds of footage captured on one passenger's mobile phone was inconclusive given the reflective glare of the train windows, but it was enough to show *something*, something of unnatural size and maybe hundreds of tiny red dots of light, and flashes of brilliant white. The incident might have gone unreported had it not been for one passenger's account, a reporter for the city's evening paper, who was quick to put his own spin on the potential headline-grabbing story Evening Gazette …

'It was as monstrous a thing as mortal man has ever laid eyes upon, a nightmarish abomination that once seen would forever scar an image in the eyes, never to be forgotten. A rat, the size of which defies nature as did everything else about it, is beyond any description this reporter can barely find the words for.

The giant rat-like creature appeared to be at the heart of a thousand smaller ones, the tails and rear parts of their bodies seemingly conjoined like some hideous equivalent of the Human Centipede cinematic character.'

London Underground and a host of government experts were quick to refute the story, calling it irresponsible and fear-mongering journalism of the worst kind, accusing the reporter of basing his article more on information from the net than on what he actually saw. Whether true or not, it wasn't enough to stop all the fringe and conspiracy magazines, journals, and online media latching onto it. To them, it provided a welcome addition to the countless other rat-related stories that were increasingly dominating International headlines, everything from super-sized rats to incredibly talented and intelligent circus rats, as another newspaper had recently reported.

As far as the mainstream press was concerned, the government took the unusual step of issuing a

D-Notice, effectively gagging them from saying another word on the matter. It was probably the last thing they should have done. Almost every person who travelled the Central line after that would spend their entire journey with their phones and faces squashed up against the train windows, eager to catch a glimpse of the alleged monster.

The authorities had been relieved that it was not to be seen again by any tube travellers, not even by those who worked and patrolled the tunnels on their nightly maintenance. But that alone was not enough to ensure the furore died. Alarming reports of people going missing in and around those areas where the underground network tunnels surfaced to the world above had increased. Tell-tale signs of blood splatters and torn clothing were an increasingly common sight around the more discreet entrances. Tunnel workers and other sub-contractors were refusing point-blank to enter them now. Again, the government was keeping a tight lid on these further developments, threatening L.U. staff with the Official Secrets Act and other dire penalties if they spoke publicly of what they knew or suspected. Something had to be done.

With or without further sightings of the underground rat monster, the government knew they had to act. COBRA protocols were initiated, namely cabinet office briefings with senior ministers, the security and intelligence services, and relevant civil servants to address not just the alleged monster of the underground but the wider rat problem too. They had also flown in leading rat expert, Dr Natalie Martins, from the Rateznox Genetics corporation to accompany the army inspections of the underground sections of London Underground. Rateznox had tried to say no at first, but the threat of suspending Rateznox's UK assets and activities was enough to make them relent.

On the pretext of purely to reassure the public that the underground metro wasn't home to rodent monsters, they took the unprecedented step of closing the entire network for several days to rid it of every last rat and whatever else might be there. The truth is that they were taking the problem very seriously. Too many knew full well that something extraordinary was happening among the rat population all around the world. They couldn't deal with every country's rat problem but were determined to stop it its tracks as far as London was concerned.

The sudden absence of the food-filled metal carriages did not go unnoticed by those living below. The King Rat was aware the two-legs were making their move against it. Long before the enemy took their first steps into the tunnels, its legion of scouts, those ones not entwined with it, would patrol the boundaries and entrances to the King Rat's world, the same ones that brought it food and new human victims.

The ones entering the tunnels were not like the usual supply of two-legs the King Rat's mobile army brought it. They walked tall and confidently. They had the look of a formidable enemy in their green camouflaged clothing, carrying what the scout rats knew to be weapons with no other purpose than to kill them. And as much as the vast underground world served to protect its rat population, it deprived them of the guerrilla tactics they would otherwise employ against the two-legs. With every entrance to their domain now blocked, they were effectively trapped as the two-legs began their slow march towards them. Whenever the rats showed themselves, they would be engulfed with shooting spears of fire, the one thing above all others the rats feared. Despite such fear, many hurled themselves at the two-legs from every dark corner in which they hid, but the two-legs were too well protected. Their boots and clothing were too thick to be penetrated by the little rats' bites and scratches, and their gas mask headgear likewise protected the two-legs' eyes and faces, the areas the rats usually favoured for their attacks. Still the rats kept coming, determined to at least slow their enemies' progress while the King Rat fled deeper into the catacombs.

"These are not the only rats down here," Dr Natalie Martins was telling the army unit she was accompanying after entering the tunnel network along the Central Line where the supposed sighting of the rat creature was first reported.

"So, you think there is something else?"

"Yes, quite definitely. Normal rat behaviour would be to flee any sight of us, something they could easily do via all the smaller drainage pipes where we can't follow. But they're deliberately sacrificing themselves to slow us down, perhaps even trying to divert us from whatever it is they're protecting."

"So, again, you give some credence to the giant rat reports?"

"Yes, I do. I can't go into specifics, but my work with Rateznox Genetics has given me access to research and knowledge of other rats much like the one alleged to exist here. The rats your men are exterminating are clearly protecting something, and that something is most likely one of their own in some form."

Dr Martins was limited in what she could tell the army officer she was speaking to, not just because of confidentiality clauses in her contract with Rateznox but also from self-preservation. A lot of the research and rat-related projects she had worked on with her employers were plain and simply illegal. She suspected too the escaped lab rats from the Rateznox laboratory that had mysteriously burnt down following the disappearance of the lab technician, Terry Stewart, might have a lot to do with the current situation, and not just in the UK.

The rat hunting carnage went on for three more days until at last the army of exterminators had something significant to report:

"We need you to come with us to the Bank area, Dr Martins. Our men think they may have found the remains of what might have been the giant rat you were referring to."

"The 'Bank' area?" she asked.

"Yes. It's one of the very deepest parts of the underground, below the central London around Bank station – but please, they need your analysis of what's been found."

Dr Martins was shown to the location the officer had spoken of. The stench was the worst she had encountered. At first glance it looked like a huge number of rats had been caught together in the flame-thrower attack on them. It puzzled her how they might have been trapped that way instead of the rats scattering in all directions. It was only examination of the rats at the edges of the apparent 'raticide' that gave her any clue. The close proximity of the charred bodies showed many them to have indeed been conjoined, both by their tails and the rear parts of their bodies as reported in the original Evening Gazette article. She observed similar though less definitive signs too towards the centre of the rodent mass.

Whatever it was, this wasn't a mass of individual rats. She dared to hope that the UK military really had killed the giant rat creature, which she knew from other such incidents was most likely a King Rat like those spoken of in folklore, only considerably bigger. Whether they had or hadn't, her report back to her Rateznox employers would say just that, that it had quite definitely been killed. Anything less, and she knew Rateznox would send their own teams of covert hunters in to try and capture the thing. She shuddered at what new experiments or creatures they might create with a real live King Rat specimen to work with.

Dr Martins needn't have worried. The King Rat had no intention of ever again being the subject of the two-legs' experiments, no matter who or what came looking for it.

*

The authorities had every reason to be pleased with themselves. The UK military had learnt valuable lessons from shared information from a similar rat-related exercise in America, where an entire town had almost been over-run by an alleged colony of super rats. Many of those soldiers had died in their clean-up operation, and significant numbers of rats were still thought to have escaped. The government had stressed to their military advisers this was not to happen in London.

There was no sign of the King Rat anywhere, other than the scorched remains of a now very dead 'abomination of nature' to paraphrase the first unofficial media report. All the long-forgotten tunnels that no human had set foot in for years had been combed, though not before several teams of flame-thrower wielding army personnel had done their worst.

All that remained of any other rats that might once have called the tunnels home were masses of virtually incinerated tiny bodies and the stomach-retching stench of burnt hair and flesh. And when they were done, vast sections of the abandoned subterranean world were sealed up after being pumped with every rat killing poison known to man before being permanently sealed.

The King Rat had sacrificed many of its legion of subordinates, having to secrete much of its paralysing saliva to deaden the responses of those rats it was entangled with. It was the only way it and those most closely conjoined could rend themselves free of the flesh of their companions.

The collective mind of the King Rat and its tail-entwined army knew they had to satisfy the two-legs that they had killed *something*. It had also been necessary to reduce its mass to escape through their own hastily dug escape route, away from any sight of the great metal carriages that hurtled through the man-made underground world. In doing so, they found their way to other parts of that world, to separate tunnels and bunkers so shrouded in secrecy that official records of their locations and even very existence had been lost.

The King Rat world had dug its own tunnels, linking the sewers, the underground, and the secret bunkers. Its surviving minions had done their part too, shifting earth and rubble behind the King Rat, sealing it off from the invading two-legged army hunting it and its followers. It now ruled an entire subterranean world, the extent of which the two-legs had no idea existed, with a lair of its own just a hundred feet below Buckingham Palace. The royalty of the rat world now sat comfortably deep beneath the two-legged royalty, it and its conjoined army slowly clawing and scratching their way upwards. With each passing hour, more rats were falling under the King Rat's control, bringing fresh meat, and helping in the digging.

It had been wise to for it to stay underground till now, burrowing as far and deep as its strength and that of its minions would allow. That was changing. The King Rat and every other type were no longer satisfied or prepared to be consigned to their sub-surface domain – they were emerging, ready to seize their place in the world above.

***

Strange Little Creatures

It was sad to think just a few weeks before they were completely free. And then the air became filled with a sleep-inducing gas. The next thing they knew they were in some alien environment, caged like wild animals.

It was that time again, no doubt another of the endless tests the giant beings had them do day after day. If they weren't navigating their way through some stupidly simple maze to earn their next meal, it would be the wheel, a circular contraption they would have to continuously run on while never actually getting anywhere. A couple of times they had chosen to stop before the bell signalling them to had rung and the rotating wheel would come to a halt. That was when they first discovered it was not wise to defy the creatures that towered over them like titans. All their captors had to do was operate a little red button, and their tiny bodies would be sent into excruciatingly painful spasms. And each time it happened, the pain increased. They had long since learned to do as they were told.

They had tried many times to communicate their intelligence, that they were more than just dumb animals for their experiments. It was no use. The difference in size made the little creatures' voices sound like unintelligible high-pitched shrieks, especially the screams whenever they were injected with some new drug or other such substance for whatever purpose. And likewise, the sounds that bellowed from their captors was like deafening thunder to them. Any hope of making themselves understood had quickly been put aside

It was useless trying to fight; quite apart from being so much smaller, their teeth and nails weren't sufficient to do much harm, even less so through the protective clothing the laboratory staff wore. The huge beings kept their strangely shaped heads covered and well protected too, making it impossible to judge their true appearance. All they could do was bide their time and hope some means of escape presented itself. It would have to be soon though. Already, several of them had disappeared, never to return. Recently, when one of the giants had left the laboratory door open, they had heard the death screams of one of their companions shortly after. They could only speculate on the manner of his death. After that, they decided they would have to engineer their own escape rather than just waiting on opportunity.

The cages they were kept in were of a simple design, the reason being that their captors never envisaged them being used for anything more than unreasoning lowly evolved animals. It never occurred to them their latest captives might be capable of so much more.

After several weeks of painstaking effort, the little creatures were able to loosen the screws holding the cage bars obstructing their freedom. It was fortunate too the shelving they were placed on had some insulated wiring running down the adjacent wall. It wasn't easy, but they were able to use it to climb down to the floor. Their diminutive size made it easy to scurry away to freedom via one of the air conditioning shafts, one that led out beyond the laboratory complex.

*

Two of the laboratory staff were discussing the new species they were studying. Physically it was similar to others found around the world, though slightly smaller in size. It was assumed these particular specimens were probably unique to the island on which they'd first been trapped. Elsewhere they were generally considered to be vermin. Every so often, the authorities would drastically cull their numbers, but these ones were different. They appeared more intelligent, with considerably less fur, like overgrown new-borns. That was why they'd been taken to the laboratory complex rather than destroyed on the spot.

"Strange and fascinating little creatures, aren't they? It's amazing how quickly they learn given their minutely sized brains."

"I agree. Though recent dissections have revealed some interesting data about them. Their brains are surprisingly complex, and actually quite large in relative to their body mass. The cerebellum is particularly well developed in this new species. I'd even say almost on a par to our own."

"I'm inclined to agree. I've been playing back amplified recordings of the sounds they make. There are numerous repetitive patterns to them, possibly the beginnings of some rudimentary form of language, though I'd be loath to admit my finding publicly without further dissections of their vocal cord regions."

*

They didn't know what sort of world that awaited them, but they were free, and that was all that mattered for now. There was a moment of joy when their tiny feet touched the soft, silk-like grass, the sun warming their bodies in a way the strictly controlled temperature of the laboratory never could.

They knew they would have to take extraordinary care. It was hard not to be afraid, knowing they were the tiniest of animals in a world of giants. The only advantage they possessed was the fact that their captors hadn't discovered just how intelligent they really were.

They were sad that only the three of them had survived long enough to escape. Oddly enough, there was no bitterness at what had happened. As scientists, they knew from experience what horrific experiments would be performed on a rival intelligent lifeform landing on Earth. They swore they would never again treat their own lab specimens in such a way should they ever find a way off this planet. They had had a taste of what it was like to be a lab specimen on the other side of the cage bars, and they hadn't liked it.

They had been aboard an interstellar freighter that had crashed on the strange planet they were now marooned. The only reason a few had survived was that they'd been enclosed in cryogenic chambers. Unfortunately, the rest of the ship had been destroyed along with all their provisions, even their clothing. They had been stranded, naked and defenceless. On the other hand, there was a breathable atmosphere, edible vegetation, and an agreeable climate. It might not be as comfortable as the colony they were heading for, but it was better than back on Earth, which was now becoming uninhabitable. They knew too there were other civilised beings on the planet, perhaps as advanced as they were. If only they could make the giants understand they were similarly intelligent, possibly even enlist their help in leaving to join their own kind. All things considered, they might just survive …

*

"You were right, they are strange little creatures. I can't say I like them though. They're selfish and self-destructive if their less evolved ones elsewhere are anything to go by. Heaven knows what they 'd be like if they weren't so small or if there were many more of them, they'd spread like cancer. God help any planet where such creatures rise to dominance. At least the ones that escaped won't get far."

"No, that's a certainty. I almost feel sorry for the creatures. It was clever of them to escape like they did, but the hunter rats will make quick meals of them."

"I imagine so," the laboratory technician chuckled, "they may be a throwback to our past, but they do a great job of helping keep the vermin numbers in check. Still, we'll need to revise our security and containment measures for any others that might be discovered in the future."

*

The human castaways had found what they thought would be the ideal place to set up camp. Lots of natural foliage to take cover in and a nearby stream for water. And food too, the biggest berries and fruit they had ever seen. It was a natural paradise for the local wildlife.

It was less than an hour before that same local wildlife noticed them. The hunter rats thought they had driven the last of the little creatures to extinction in their local hunting grounds. The rodent predators circled them, ready to pounce on the tiny two-legged meals. Their whiskers were twitching in anticipation; berries and fruit were tasty and nutritious, but nothing could beat the taste and smell of live food.

It was easy for them to fall on upon their next meal. Though nowhere near the size of the dominant *Rattus Superior* mischief, they were still three times the size of their intended prey.

There would soon be three less vermin on the planet of the rats ...

*

Back on Earth ...

'... *Reports of the interstellar transport colony ship, Horizon, being lost are coming in. It's now known it never reached its destination in sector 12. It must be assumed the crew and passengers are now lost. It is hoped they managed to land on one of the other friendly life-supporting planets en route ...*'

***

And the Rats shall Inherit the Earth ...

It was three in the morning when Anthony Johnson reluctantly scrambled out from under his warm duvet. His bed was in the attic bedroom, enabling him to enjoy the view of the stars through the skyline window. The only drawback was having to navigate the steep stairway if he needed to use the bathroom in the middle of the night.

Like countless others at the time, he'd been horrified when confronted with the mass of fur crawling about his home. He knew immediately what they were - living in the country, rats and all sorts were part and parcel of living on the outskirts of a forest. But a few traps, regular checks, and treatment of the outer walls and foundations were usually enough to keep them at bay ... until now. He had no idea how they had got in, but he could hear more of them scratching at the walls, the front door, the windows, and from all around the log cabin. He reached for his cell-phone to call 911. There was no answer, just a repeated message saying that their switchboards were receiving an unusually high number of calls.

More rats were emerging from the kitchen area and from behind various pieces of furniture. He turned back towards the attic stairway, hoping to climb out of their reach but they were already there, scurrying about the lower steps. Without warning, they started biting at his feet and ankles. The sudden pain took him by surprise, and he fell to the floor. Except for his boxer shorts, Anthony Johnson was naked, making it easier for them to attack every part of his body.

Dozens swarmed over his body, biting, scratching, ripping away at his skin and the underlying flesh, hundreds of razor-sharp teeth eating him alive. The only benefit, if you could call it that, was that Anthony Johnson died quickly. The swiftness of his death was no deliberate act of mercy though. They were eager to move onto a hundred others just like him.

Living where he did, ironically, should have lessened the likelihood of the rats paying Anthony Johnson any attention that night. It was the urban centres of population they had concentrated on, the humans most essential to keeping society going. But his edge of the forest location had been convenient for his experimental work at the 101 facility where so many rats had met their deaths. That had made him a special case for the rats …

Martha Evans lived on the twenty-seventh floor of a luxury residential block. The views were stunning, and more importantly, it distanced her from the hustle and bustle of the busy New York streets below; even in her affluent neighbourhood, the streets were awash with crime, and she was glad to be away from it in the safety of her swish apartment hundreds of feet up. Another consideration had been her loathing of the rats that had become such a problem in the city over recent years. The real estate man had assured Martha that was one problem she'd never have to worry about ... unless of course they ever grew wings.

The rats hadn't needed to grow wings. Instead, some found their way into the elevator shafts, hitching rides just feet away from the humans beneath the underside of the elevator ceilings. Many more had scrambled their way up the emergency fire stairways in the dead of night over the past week, settling themselves in any hidden corner they could find, waiting ...

Virtually the entire apartment block awoke at the same time as if every telephone had rung along with every TV and radio being turned to full volume. It was neither of those things. The noise was the same everywhere, the sound of screams as people realised what was happening was no nightmare.

Martha's own scream was just one of the

city-wide chorus at 3.05 am that morning when the first rat crawled over her face. Others were crawling about her body after she had thrown off the bedding in her sleep because of how warm the night was. The flimsy silk material of her negligée would be no defence to their teeth and claws. Her first scream had just been one of sudden realisation. The second one barely a moment later was louder and more urgent. It was one of pain. Two razor-sharp incisors had sunk their way into the soft flesh of one of her eyes. Martha sprang from her bed only to immediately fall to the ground, paralysed by more slashing at the lower tendons at the back of her ankles. It would have been easy for her to just curl up in a foetal position and wait for the inevitable end as the rats finished their attack, but Martha's horror of the revolting and hideous creatures compelled her to try and escape their onslaught. A pain-driven adrenalin surge enabled her to partially ignore the barrage of bites and scratches the rats were inflicting. She frantically crawled and pulled her way towards her apartment balcony door. Martha had hoped to take refuge there if she could only manage to slam the balcony door shut behind her. It was a hopeless task of course. Adrenalin and determination alone were no antidote to the rapid loss of blood she was suffering. She died to the sound of both her own and countless other screams echoing from adjacent apartments and the streets far below …

Gil Richards was coming towards the end of his shift. He loved his job driving trains for the New York City Subway, just not in the early hours of the morning.

67th Avenue station on the Queens Boulevard line was not far ahead. It alarmed Gil that he could still see the rear lights of another train in the distance. He was sure it would soon start to move but nonetheless, slowly began to apply the brake. Just as he was he was about to call his control on the train radio, the biggest rat Gil had ever seen leapt to the Dead-Man's handle safety device he was holding down. Apart from the likelihood of a fright-induced heart attack, his initial reaction was to recoil in horror and snatch his hand away. The train screeched as the emergency brake immediately sought to bring the train to a halt as the Dead-Man's handle did its work. Gil in the meantime was in a panic. Two more rats were scurrying about his feet. None of his emergency-situation training had covered the present scenario. Amid the confusion, he looked ahead. The other train was still there, and his own hadn't slowed sufficiently yet to avoid running into the back of it. In the event of an unavoidable collision, a train driver would usually have exited back into the carriage, urging passengers to move as far back as they could, but these were nothing like usual circumstances. Everything was happening so quickly, and Gil was still in a partial state of shock from the sudden appearance of several rats in his driving cab.

It wasn't a full-speed collision, but fast enough to crumble the impact ends of both trains. Gil was killed instantly. Perhaps that was a good thing – it spared him the sight of other dead bodies strewn about the station platform, and from seeing hundreds more rats running this way and that among the few early morning passengers and staff that hadn't yet been brought down by the mass of rodent killers. They weren't to survive long …

*

October 15th was what became known as *The Night of the Long Teeth*, the day/night that was to change the world forever. Never before had so many died in such a short space of time.

It was the speed and coordination that had shocked what was left of the world. It was a blitzkrieg the like of which could not otherwise have been imagined, utterly dwarfing that of the German tanks that had once rampaged across Europe or the Japanese attack on Pearl Harbour.

In the space of a single night, or day depending on where you were, rats had simultaneously attacked human population centres across the world. It was in the cities and larger towns where the attacks were felt the worst, particularly where it was night or the early hours of the morning when people were at their most vulnerable. Most had been attacked in their beds while they slept.

For weeks, the rats had been preparing, ferrying supplies to sustain them while they amassed their numbers in basements, cellars, crawl and roof spaces, even the empty space between walls. Untold numbers had climbed up lift-shafts, hiding in every nook and cranny that could accommodate them. And then they waited.

In those regions where it was still light, more attacks had been directed towards the smaller towns, those with few tall buildings that the rats could not so easily scale or hide in, especially without the shield of darkness to aid them. But the cities did not go unscathed. To coordinate their daytime attacks with the night ones in other parts of the world, the daylight attacks had to be more imaginative. The rat legions ignored the very young and elderly, they could be dealt with later – it was the healthy adult humans they directed their assaults, the ones most likely to cause them problems in the future.

Knowing most would be awake and going about their usual business, the rats adopted different tactics. They hid in the humans' cars, their trains, and in places where humans worked alone or were few in number, everywhere they could wreak the most havoc.

They attacked en masse at key points while others sacrificed themselves running into busy city roads to cause traffic accidents. Ninety-five per cent of the attacks were coordinated to occur within a few minutes of one another, such was the military precision of the rats' planning.

While most humans had died from direct attacks, millions more were killed in plane and train crashes when rats attacked the pilots and drivers, or when air traffic control centres and signal boxes likewise found themselves overrun with swarming blankets of black and brown fur. It was the same on the roads too, car drivers going into a blind panic at the shock of a rat suddenly nipping at their ankles while their feet were still on the gas and brake pedals.

Not long after the first Rateznox orchestrated decimation, the world rat population had been severely underestimated. Despite almost half falling to the Rateznox poisons, the rats' ability to breed at such phenomenal rates allowed them to quickly repopulate.

At the start of the attack, the rats had already grown their numbers to the point where they outnumbered their human enemy by a ratio of three to two. By the end of the day, that ratio was more like three to one – more than 4 billion men, woman, and children had died in the space of just a few hours

The new generations were very different breeds. It was no longer just a case of the standard brown and black varieties. The escaped lab rats from England had become dominant now. They were longer lived, enabling an almost exponential explosion in their numbers. Most frightening though was their seemingly psychic abilities combined with measurable IQ levels of intelligence. They could communicate telepathically far more efficiently than any of the human methods of remote communication and had used their 'abilities' to marshal the other new breeds to their cause.

Much of the war had many of the characteristics of a conventional conflict – initial tensions, minor skirmishes to start, conflicting needs and ambitions of the opposing sides, then an escalation to open attacks. The only thing missing had been a formal declaration as such, it was hardly that sort of war. The two-legs had been loath to admit such a state of affairs with an enemy so much smaller and less intelligent than themselves (or so they desperately wanted to believe).

While many in the scientific community suspected, only the Rateznox Genetics corporation had known the true extent of the potential threat the rats posed. They had kept quiet out of self-interest, determined not to reveal the part they had played in escalating that threat. It had been a costly mistake. Dr Natalie Martins had been right, the Rateznox share price was the least of anyone's worries now.

Despite the horrific death toll and resultant chaos in the days that followed, humanity was far from finished in those early days. With their attack over, the rats no longer had the element of surprise on their side, and their two-legged enemy was quick to respond. Little thought was given to the broader civilian population, they would have to fend for themselves. What was left of the military and governments around the world set up rat-free quarantine zones for anyone who reached them to take refuge. Vast areas and even entire towns were cleared of their rat populations. Many were to die in what became known as the second great rat clearance.

The rats had expected such a response and were prepared for their losses, knowing they could replace their numbers far quicker than their human enemy. In the meantime, they set about finishing off the rural two-legged communities, the ones that couldn't reach the rat-free quarantine zones. Most cars and lorries had had their tyres ripped to shreds by the rural rat population, thus further preventing escape to the rat-free zones.

The rats weren't concerned with attacking their enemy now, they didn't have to. Most would die of starvation given the state of siege they were now in and the complete breakdown of the two-legs' society and infrastructure.

From their bunkers and rat-free zones, remnants of government and local authority called emergency meetings on how to deal with the situation, still clinging to the belief it was the beginning of the war rather than its end. Others too called their own meetings in those cities and facilities that had escaped the worst of the attack. One such meeting was attended by the remaining executives of the Rateznox Genetics corporation ...

"We've sold our bill of goods just a little too well," Dr Natalie Martins was telling the Rateznox panel, and not without a smug tone of 'I told you so.'

"Now is not the time for recrimination. We can still turn the situation around. We just need to refine the RN249 serum, and we can get rid of the rats once and for all. That will be part of your job, Dr Martins."

"Me? No way. I'm done with all this. As soon as I walk out from here, I'm taking off as far away as possible. With a bit of luck, the rats will have had their fill of us, though who really knows with the mutant abominations we've created."

"In case you've forgotten, you're still under contract, Dr Martins."

"That's fine," she replied, practically laughing at the absurdity of their reminder. Society had collapsed all around them, and Rateznox was threatening her with employment law: "You can sue me for breach of contract."

Unlike at previous summons to appear before the Rateznox board, Natalie Martins wasn't afraid this time. The implicit threat of not coming out alive no longer had any teeth to it. Most of Rateznox's security thugs had died along with billions of others the rats had attacked that night. Indeed, her only reason for bothering to turn up at all was curiosity and a desire to finally tell them what a crazy bunch of scientifically ignorant fucks they were. In the end, she didn't bother and just walked, oblivious to their angry tirade. She had no idea just where she was going, but with her knowledge of the rats, she had a better chance of survival than most.

*

Any thought of resurrecting human society to its former splendour was soon abandoned. In the space of a few years following what had become known as the night of the long teeth, another two billion were to slowly die without the complicated infrastructure most of the world had relied on.

As far as humans were concerned, the war had by most definitions been lost. There were still pockets of resistance scattered across the world and even an uneasy peace where there had been a history of friendly co-existence, where rats and humans continued to live the same way. But such areas were rare, the famous Karni Mata temple of the rats being one of the few. The humans there had worshipped a strange and a mysterious warrior breed of rat for many centuries. The now dominant genetically enhanced strain that had been set free by the British lab assistant, Terry Stewart, were wary of them. Their encounter with Ratcula and others of the blood creatures had given the enhanced lab rats cause to be afraid of anything that so much as hinted of the supernatural. There were others too that worried them – the super rats of America for one, whose numbers greatly exceeded their own in that land. Their American cousins didn't share the lab rats' greater intelligence or mental abilities, but they were bigger and stronger, possessing a degree of aggression that frightened them. Nor did their larger cousins show the same deference as did what could still be called 'normal' rats.

The ones they feared the most though were the mutant abominations, those rats sharing genes with all manner of creatures. Most of the mutants had died, but not all. There still existed the giant ravenous monster of the sewers, the one that had once lived in Terry Stewart's cellar. And then there was the most monstrous of them all, the original King Rat of Sumatra.

Not all rats were created equal, and the lab rats had inherited the world. But they had rivals for the keeping of it ... *another war was coming.*

***

Evolution

Not only had the age of man been and gone, it was now forgotten and with little left to barely hint of its existence. Not a trace remained of the vast cities and infrastructure that once scarred the planet, both above and below the surface. The dominant species of the present day had no need for such things. Everything the humans had once been able to do, so too could *Rattus superior*, some with their minds and others physically, though, in truth, they were so very different that any meaningful comparison was near impossible.

The rats would often find remnants of human technology, but they were rarely of interest. Still though, occasionally a fossil would emerge which attracted their attention, as had been the case recently since the thawing of the great ice sheets.

An island had revealed itself just below one of the retreating glaciers. Again, such things seldom drew the attention of the different rat species, they had all the land and space they needed, but the predator rats were always excited by the possibility of new hunting grounds, and many had migrated there.

The six-foot predator rat, a descendant of the tiny

and now long extinct brown Norway rat, *Rattus norvegicus*, puzzled over the skull it had unearthed. It was unlike anything it had seen before, circular instead of the more elongated ones of its own and other related species. Surprising too was the small and almost non-existent shape of the mouth, too small to house flesh-rending teeth to eat or defend itself. It was little wonder such a species had become extinct, the predator rat mused. Still, it was an intriguing find, one that might interest the 'thinking' ones.

With its blazing red eyes, the smaller albino rat, one of what the predator and other rats called the thinking ones, observed the curious fossil its larger relation had brought it. Unlike the predator, this one recognised the fossil for what it was, the skull of a creature that was now just an inherited memory of an almost forgotten past. Only the strongest minds of the thinking ones could draw on the pool of genetic memory their kind possessed.

It was remarkably intact from having been preserved in the recently thawed ice. The rat sniffed and brushed its whiskers over it. A hundred thousand years old, it judged, though it would take a much closer examination to draw out all the ancient fossil's secrets. The thinking one ordered the predators to search for other such fossils about the island where it had been found. They soon had a dozen more such skulls and other skeletal remains, all equally well preserved. The little albino rat's whiskers quivered in anticipation at what might be learned from them.

It called for others of its kind to help. A dozen more minds joined in probing what temporal energy they still possessed.

Being able to read a fossil's past was just one of the thinking ones' amazing abilities. They had evolved over tens of thousands of generations since the first stirrings of their psychic abilities, which were now as far advanced as 21st-century technology was in comparison to stone age man. Their powers weren't without limit though. Had the fossil been some other part of the skeleton to which it once belonged, the clarity of what they could learn from it would have been cloudy and fragmented. But a fully intact skull was something else. With its former proximity to the brain and thoughts of the body it once belonged to, the rats would be able to see into the very mind and memories of its now long deceased owner. And the other remains too would provide an even wider and more accurate picture of the island's past inhabitants …

The words and image of a man began to form, and the rats watched and listened while a dramatic period of the subject's life started to take shape … His name was Simon …

Simon Vale, Professor of paelobiology at Cambridge University was not impressed when he read one of the tabloids' reactions to his address to the World Environmental and Futures conference in Geneva that year ...

'... *You can forget horse-riding super-intelligent apes or the rise of the cockroaches after a nuclear war, it'll be super-sized rats the size of elephants that will inherit the earth to become our new lords and masters.*'

The idiots, Simon thought. He'd said nothing about cockroaches or any of the other nonsense they'd written in their rag of a newspaper. Scepticism was to be expected, even outright disbelief, but not the level of scorn they'd poured on his predictions.

Much of his research and its conclusions were almost always open to interpretation, especially given their speculative elements. It had always frustrated the professor that his work could so often be disputed, and as had happened at the conference, ridiculed.

This time was different, the stakes were so much higher. It wouldn't have been so bad if they'd responded with solid evidence to refute his claims. On this occasion, it would have been the most enormous relief to be proved wrong.

He understood why they hadn't been believed

him though. It was hard to believe it himself, and not just because of how extraordinary his claims were. The implications were beyond anything Simon Vale could imagine, but more than that, he didn't *want* to believe. Given a choice, no sane person would. He wished he could turn the clock back …

"Well there it is, the conclusive proof we needed, Simon," Laura Hathaway was telling her colleague.

Laura Hathaway had fed all the professor's data and research into her computer simulation model. Everything pointed to an alarming set of conclusions. A perfect storm of circumstances was combining to alter the evolutionary destiny of two of the three most successful species on the planet.

"I can see that!" Simon snapped, instantly regretting his abrupt response. It wasn't her fault; as a fellow scientist, he knew there was no way she could dress up their findings to make them any the more palatable. But still, it was hard having to face the certainty of the planet's dominant species being superseded by one that spent the greater part of their lives scavenging among human left-overs rather than changing the world with their cutting-edge technology.

"We can stop it," Simon continued, "we know the factors that are driving this, it's not too late."

He didn't believe his own words any more than Laura did. His resolve was just a knee-jerk reaction to the truth, trying to convince himself nothing was inevitable about their predictions. In theory that was true. A world-wide effort might indeed avert mankind's simulated future. But what chance of that? The industrialised nations were still burning up the planet just so their citizens could drive to the supermarket instead of walk, wasting trillions of watts of energy merely to illuminate the night, or to keep the air-conditioning running 24/7.

Even with the consequences staring them in the face, mankind was continuing its path of self-destruction. So again, what chance of it taking any notice of one lone paelobiologist and a computer programmer's fantastical claims that it might, no, *would* be replaced by creatures whose size and intelligence was so far beneath us? But those last aspects were changing. Rats were continuing to fill the newly available ecospace in the wake of the continuing extinctions of other mammalian species, especially the larger ones. Parallel to this, with their larger rivals out of the way, evolutionary gigantism was being observed among the rats as they filled ever larger niches of the environment, just as the disappearance of the dinosaurs allowed their tiny mammalian successors the opportunity to grow and exploit their absence.

In simpler terms, the rats were getting bigger and smarter. Until now, rats had been the most successful and adaptable species on the planet behind insects and then humans. Not an island or continent remained free of one sort of rodent or another. And while diversity among mankind was being eroded, every island and tiniest corner the rats inhabited was serving as an evolutionary laboratory for their development. They were now on the verge of moving up from third to second place in that order.

Just a few weeks before, Simon and Laura like most people had mixed thoughts as to the future. As scientists, it was easy for them to believe some of the wild predictions, courtesy of YouTube documentaries: being enslaved by Artificial Super Intelligence, nuclear war, a devastating flu pandemic, or more optimistically, heaven on earth thanks to the wonders of science – they were all plausible possibilities. But that's all they were – possibilities, and remote ones at that. The coming horror was far from remote.

They had checked and re-checked their findings, each time becoming more convinced they were right yet still desperate to interpret the slightest indication they weren't.

*

It was the 16th October, the day after 'the night of long teeth' that had proved some of the truth of

Simon and Laura's findings, even while the rodent legions were still inflicting their vicious worldwide attacks.

It had been clear the rats would eventually make some sort of move to assert themselves. Simon just hadn't anticipated the scale or it happening in his own lifetime.

On the night of the long teeth, Simon had been visiting a remote island just off the coast of Sumatra, observing and collecting rat specimens for comparison with others he'd obtained and seen elsewhere around the world. Unbeknown to him then, it was also the same island where Rateznox Genetics had set up and its secret and controversial research facilities for their gene-splicing experiments. It was where they had created the worst of the rat mutations and hybrids, not that Simon saw much evidence of that, at least not at first.

Most of the rogue genetics company's unnatural creations had attacked their keepers that night and escaped into to the safety of the dense island jungle. Even after the rats' epic victory over their human masters, they kept their distance while they assumed mastery of their new environment.

*

Knowing the chaos going on elsewhere, a remote

island would be a good place to live and continue his work, Simon decided. It had its own generator and suitable laboratory facilities for his research, all within a fenced compound. If nothing else, at least the rats there were isolated from what was going on in the rest of the world was his reasoning, unaware of the rat horrors of the jungle, biding their time out of sight.

He was glad too that his friend and colleague, Dr Natalie Martins, had agreed to join him just as soon as she could now that her contract with Rateznox Genetics was no longer a problem. Sadly, not all his friends and colleagues had survived the night of the long teeth. Laura Hathaway was one of the billions that died during those 24 hours of carnage.

Simon Vale watched as the luxury yacht navigated its way into the only safe berthing dock on the island for a vessel of that size.

"Great to have you with us, Dr Martins," Simon greeted, "though I've got to say, I wasn't expecting such a grand arrival."

"Courtesy of my former employers, Professor Vale. With all the confusion going on, I used my position to commandeer one of our corporate hospitality yachts on the pretext of critical overseas research. I just neglected to mention I'd already resigned, and the research had nothing to do with

Rateznox Genetics," Natalie joked, "and I managed to round up a few personnel with me, and the crew of course."

"Actually, I hardly think academic titles matter anymore," Simon laughed, "are they all staying?"

"Yes. Like you, *Simon*, they all figure an island is a better bet compared to what's happening on the mainland. And what's more, the yacht's chock full of the supplies and equipment you asked for."

"Thanks, they'll be an immense help. Oh, and it's good to have you with us too."

"Glad to be here. But how much do you know about this island? I mean, were you aware Rateznox Genetics had one of their own facilities based here? This might not be quite the haven you think it is."

"No, I wasn't. But where? I've seen no sign of it."

"It's the other side of the jungle. They used to supply it by small motor launches from larger vessels berthed out at sea. I've got the file on it with me."

*

Deep in the jungle on the other side of the island, the escaped monstrosities of Dr Natalie Martins' former employers were quickly establishing their dominance over the native rat population.

There were no mountains of human left-overs for them to scavenge which meant having to hunt for their food. And unlike the humans, their fellow inhabitants of the jungle were wild, with teeth and claws every bit as deadly as their own. For the regular rat population, they were as much the hunted as the hunters. But the escaped rats were entirely different. They were vicious and easily intelligent enough to compensate for the greater strength and size of their jungle-dwelling rivals. They soon interbred with the native rats, and it was *their* mutated genes and DNA that dominated the numerous offspring.

Within six months, a new multi-hybrid breed of rat had emerged, one that's additional strength and intelligence combined with sheer weight of numbers now stood atop the jungle hierarchy.

Most were several times the size of their native cousins, some even bigger. They tended to stand on their larger hind-legs much of the time, giving the appearance of mini kangaroos but with a head and face more like something out of the Jurassic period. And the front limbs and hands were more dexterous, much like man's early transition from dragging its knuckles to full bipedalism. They didn't yet have anywhere near the cerebral development of their

British lab-rat cousins, but they were fast catching up. It was only a matter of time before they outgrew their new jungle domain.

*

The Rateznox Genetics' files and research Natalie Martins had shared with Simon made for disturbing reading. If he'd had it at the time he and Laura were putting together their evolutionary predictions for the future, he probably wouldn't have been so surprised at the events of the 15th October.

Simon Vale had been hopeful that with Natalie's and that of the other researchers' help they'd be able to come up with a biological solution to the rat problem, albeit somewhat late in the day. Natalie was quick to scupper that idea in its tracks: "We can forget about coming up with some magic-bullet type poison for them. They've evolved whole new genes to help them detoxify chemicals and toxins in the livers and other parts of their bodies. Living in the sewers, pipes, and just about every other harsh or unsanitary environment you can think of has propelled their evolution adaptability way faster than ours or any other creature's.

"You understand? It wasn't just animal genes and DNA they were combining with the rats,' but human too."

Simon paused at Natalie's revelation. Genetics wasn't really his field and found it hard to believe half what had been done was even possible.

"It was never about how difficult it was, Simon. You see, we share over 95 per cent of genes and DNA with the different rat species. Much of it's what we call junk or lying dormant. We even share genes that enable us to grow tails, though in humans it's not 'switched on.' And vice versa, we have active genes that in the rats are switched off. So again, there's are huge areas of potential development for them, and enough genetic overlap between us for Rateznox to have proceeded with much of their far-fetched research. And before you say it, yes, I was a part of that."

"Don't worry, I'm not going to reproach you on that. I already know the methods Rateznox used to coerce their employers along controversial research lines. But the idea of rat/human hybrids of whatever degree, apart from horrifying, it's disgusting. What were they thinking of?" All Natalie could do was shrug at Simon's question.

On the other side of the island, the Rateznox staff were all dead, killed and eaten by their own creations. Though the new breeds of rat owed their increased strength and intelligence to their former masters, they remembered too at what price; the painful experiments, the live dissections, and the very worst of their sibling creations. Such was the deformity and hideousness of many of them, the more successful and viable resultant rats had quickly killed the Rateznox failures. They would likely have soon died anyway, but such was the absolute wretchedness of the lives, it was a mercy to put them out of their misery. Such creatures had no part to play in the rats' destiny, but they deserved to be avenged for having been brought into the world at all.

The hybrid rats' numbers had now stabilised. They knew the island jungle could not sustain much further growth, but they still had many new litters to feed.

They now occupied every corner of the jungle. The hybrid rats were too large to get too close without being spotted. Just one of their gene-spliced abilities was cat-like eyesight, so they watched the new human arrivals on the far-side of their island kingdom from a safe distance.

At first, the humans had only been a minor curiosity. There were only a dozen or so they could see, hardly enough to pose a threat. For a while, the humans remained unaware of the watching rats' presence which is how it might have stayed.

It was the rat traps that alerted the new hybrids to the humans' activities. They were like the other ones, experimenting on them, probably killing them too, the rats assumed. That changed everything.

The rats started to watch them more closely, less concerned now at being seen. There were enough of their two-legged enemies feed several litters till they were mature enough to hunt their own food. There was also the undoubted supplies they would have brought them. Humans had no capacity for individual survival. Virtually cut off from their more extensive human mischief, they would make for easy and deserved victims.

*

"Yes, I've seen them too, Simon, but only their tracks so far."

"Same here, Natalie, and a couple of the others have reported spotting something more when checking the rat traps. And what's more, we've not successfully captured a single rat in weeks now."

"What do you mean, 'successfully'?"

"Most of the traps were exactly as I left them, but a couple had clearly worked. There was evidence of rat droppings, tracks etc. but the traps had been broken into. I've no idea what could do that. Here, let me show what I mean."

Simon showed her one of the traps. Its roof and

sides had been torn apart, and judging from the damage, with ease.

"Some other animal wanting an easy meal would be my first thought, but no, I can't think of any native animal with the dexterity to rip a trap apart quite like that."

"We need a live specimen of whatever did this, Natalie, and to know just how much bigger they're likely to get. Mine and Laura's predictions weren't predicting this sort of evolution for decades, or centuries more like. But the addition of human genes and DNA in the rodent genome changes everything."

"Even with a live specimen, I'd need additional equipment for the sort of tests I'd need to do, Simon."

"What about the Rateznox lab, wouldn't they be likely to have what you need?"

"Well, yes, but we don't have a motor launch, and there's nowhere to berth a yacht the size of ours. And given what else might have escaped from the lab, I certainly don't fancy the idea of trekking through the jungle to it. It'll have to be the mainland."

Natalie, two other researchers, and three crew members took the Rateznox yacht and set sail. Meanwhile, Simon and the others on the island set about figuring how to capture one of the creatures that had broken the traps designed to catch the native rats. It couldn't be a regular trap given the suspected size of whatever it was that was out there. A pit was decided upon, something deep enough that would prevent escape, they hoped.

The area around them was too flat and open for what they had in mind. For any chance of success, it would have to be farther away, just within the nearest outskirts of the nearby jungle. They dug three such pits around some dead meat from their supplies for bait. The rats were more than capable of hunting their own food, Simon knew, but when presented with the prospect of free food without any effort there was a good chance they would catch at least one of the creatures they were after.

Simon and his colleagues were careful to obscure what they were up to for fear of the rats seeing what they were up to. It was hardly likely too that whatever they hoped to catch would be so accommodating as to willingly jump in, so it was necessary to disguise the pits with light bracken and foliage.

It was then just a matter of waiting and watching …

It was almost a week before the yacht returned, this time with a small motor launch aboard should they wish to visit the other side of the island. It was not all they had brought with them.

They had lost radio contact with the island during the trip back, so there was no grand reception for the yacht this time, in fact, no reception at all. Thankfully it was less than half a mile from the berthing dock and where Simon had his lab and the facility where they all lived.

The six of them started to make their way back with the equipment and supplies they had brought. They didn't notice the small compliment of stowaways that had hitched a ride with them back to the island.

"Where is everyone? The whole place looks deserted," one of the yacht crew remarked.

"I wish I knew," was all Natalie could say, "let's get the gear and supplies inside and we'll see where they are," she added, hoping to briefly take everyone's mind off the apparently deserted compound.

The compound gate was locked, so maybe the others were off on some sort of expedition? It was all Natalie could think of, hoping to god she was right. It wasn't long before she began to have her doubts. It was immediately clear something was wrong. All the tinned and dried food supplies were gone. The lab and living quarters were in a mess too, like they had been ransacked. And there was no sign of Simon or the others to be found.

"They had no way of leaving the island while we were away, and I doubt they would have gone even if another boat had berthed in the meantime, not without leaving us a message."

"You're right, they wouldn't," Natalie agreed. "That just leaves the jungle. The only reason for venturing through it would be to try and reach the Rateznox lab on the far side of the island for whatever reason. And assuming they made it, I think we should take the yacht to investigate. If we don't find them, then we'll head back to the mainland."

Had they looked further, Natalie and the others would have found their colleagues. The rats had not been fooled by the rat-catching pits. Instead, they had indeed jumped willingly into them and waited for their would-be captors to arrive. They didn't have to wait long. As soon as the humans came for them, they had leapt from the pits and set about their hated enemy, dragging three of them down into the very prisons they had dug. All that was left were their bones and ragged clothing after the rats had had their fill of them. The remaining humans they dragged through into the heart of the jungle to feed their growing and hungry offspring. Other rats dug their way beneath the compound perimeter fencing to scavenge whatever supplies the humans might have left. It would have been better for Natalie and the crew to have suffered the same fate than what awaited them on the other side of the island ...

The motor launch berthed on the stretch of beach nearest the Rateznox facility. Scout rats watched Natalie and the crew's arrival, knowing that would be the place any intruding humans would come from. They knew too it would be the laboratory where the white-coated humans had once kept and tortured many of their kind that they would head for. They did nothing to stop them, keeping well out of sight so's not to alert the humans to their presence. The scout rats scurried off to warn their smaller cousins of the humans' imminent arrival.

The compliment of tiny stowaways that had hidden aboard the Rateznox yacht were offspring of the more intelligent and seemingly psychic lab rats that escaped from a similar Rateznox facility back in England. They had used the humans' ocean-going cargo ships to quickly spread across the world, eventually boarding the Rateznox yacht to reach the island they all now found themselves on. They had cut through the island jungle to reach the white-coated humans' laboratory well ahead of Natalie and her party.

There was now an even more powerful genus of *Rattus* on the island, one far in advance of anything even Simon Vale had conceived of. It was somewhat smaller than the larger recently evolved predatory hybrid there, though still surprisingly stronger and faster than any of the remaining native rats. But this new breed wasn't just smarter, they had *real* intelligence comparable to any of the two-legs. These latest rats to the island knew too they owed this to the white-coated humans' experiments on them, experiments they knew and understood, not just from observing them, but probing their enemies' minds.

They had wondered how they might continue those experiments, awakening all those dormant psychic genes and human DNA, propelling their rapid evolution even further.

They now had several new human subjects to work with.

*

It had been a remarkable story, and a disturbing one too. Collectively, the humans of old had been a hated enemy, one that had tried to exterminate them innumerable times just as they had successfully done so many other species. And yet, the rats owed their abilities and much of evolutionary development to them. Were it not for the two-legged creatures, they might still be just another tiny part in the food chain, and one much lower down instead of their ruling position at the top. This much they already knew, but they had learnt something new … If not the actual descendants, they were now in part, another species of man.

There was so much more now the rats wanted to know, to fill the long dark gaps in their inherited memories. They would search for more human skulls to learn the full truth of their shared history with the extinct two-legs …

The End … *for now.*

***

To be continued in the forthcoming novels:

The Plague Years: A Rat Tales Novel

The Night of the Long Teeth: A Rat Tales Novel

The Rodent Wars: A Rat Tales Novel

A word from the author ...

Reviews and customer comments are the lifeblood of independent authors, so if you enjoyed this book, or not as the case may be, might I ask that you take a minute or two to leave a brief review on either Amazon, Goodreads, or another such review site.

Such reviews and feedback help authors gauge what their readers might like in the future, as well as helping promote their work to new readers.

Many thanks,

P.A. Rudders

P.A.RUDDERS

Printed in Great Britain
by Amazon